PALE ORCHID

Bethany delays her hopes of rescuing a failing relationship while she helps a friend by working at The Corner Cattery. But there are unexpected problems. She becomes involved with twin brothers and the bitter feud between them: Dominic the successful but troubled and moody playwright; Darryl the dedicated doctor torn between his work in Africa and his two motherless children. Many conflicts must be resolved, and searching questions answered, before Bethany can see clearly her road ahead.

MAVIS THOMAS

PALE ORCHID

Complete and Unabridged

LINFORD
Leicester

First published in Great Britain in 2008

First Linford Edition
published 2009

British Library CIP Data

Thomas, Mavis.
    Pale orchid- -(Linford romance library)
    1. Love stories.
    2. Large type books.
    I. Title II. Series
    823.9'2–dc22

    ISBN 978–1–84782–720–3

Published by
F. A. Thorpe (Publishing)
Anstey, Leicestershire
Set by Words & Graphics Ltd.
Anstey, Leicestershire
Printed and bound in Great Britain by
T. J. International Ltd., Padstow, Cornwall

This book is printed on acid-free paper

1

The snow had started just after breakfast. It was still snowing. Not what you would call a dramatic white-out, but it hadn't helped the drive down from my parents' home near Leicester. Now I had reached this final stage of the journey, south of London, the main roads here were a slushy mess under a sullen grey sky.

Homebound schoolchildren, of that category scorning coats, were dawdling in their unfastened blazers and shivery mini-skirts. Elderly folk, bent-shouldered, plodded grimly on with shopping bags.

I turned off the irritatingly cheery chat on the car radio. There wasn't too much to be cheery about! Really I shouldn't be here at all on this last-minute emergency errand, but bound instead for Paris, France, to see Toby . . . and to discover whether his ring on my finger still meant anything to either of us.

'Right at the station, then straight on, you can't miss us!' Mrs. Garland had told me on the phone this morning. It sounded all right then, but I wasn't so sure now. It was quite a while since I last came here on a flying visit — before I started nursing at the Mid-Counties Park Hospital, before I met Toby.

'Right at the station, keep on going,' I muttered aloud. Things weren't looking good when you conversed with yourself at age twenty-six, on a day that should be spring but resembled Siberian mid-winter. 'Keep straight on, keep going . . .'

And there suddenly was my destination looming out of the murk, a corner house at the junction of three roads: not large, but boasting a spacious spread of triangular garden, hidden away behind high walls and a tall gate. A board on the wall announced: *THE CORNER CATTERY* — *Visitors please ring bell.*

I wasn't exactly a visitor. I had come

in answer to a plea for help from my long time friend Michelle Garland. Just when I was all set for Paris and Toby, she had phoned me to beg a big favour: her fiancé Trevor, en route to his grandparents in Devon, had been involved in a serious motorbike smash-up and was badly injured. She couldn't wait to reach his hospital bedside. However, that meant leaving the Cattery — a joint venture with her widowed mother, which had proved very successful — for the moment in Mrs. Garland's sole care. Not a good idea, because Grace Garland, with the best of intentions, would smother the boarders with hugs and forget to order new supplies of food or litter.

'But I'm not sure I'd do much better,' I had demurred despite all my sympathy. 'I've never had any dealings with animals.'

'You're a nurse, aren't you? You'll cope!' was her response to that. 'It might be just a few days, I'm praying it will. If it looks like being longer — well, we'll have to think again.'

How could I refuse? Ten years ago we were at school together, always in and out of each other's homes, sharing shopping sprees, panics over exams. Despite our destinies and locations varying since then, always we had kept in close touch, even though of late not in face-to-face contact.

So I was here today, at the start of my three weeks saved-up leave, reporting for whatever dubious duties awaited me. And the very first problem was to park. Eventually I slotted in, with inches to spare, among a haphazard line of snow-whitened vehicles.

The place had altered since I was last here, when the Cattery was newly acquired and opened. Now, there was additional security, an answer-phone contact by the big gate, a notice about opening hours 'Strictly By Appointment'. But the separate entrance to the house was unchanged. I dragged my big suitcase on its clogged-up wheels to the front door.

'Bethany, you've got here! It's so lovely to see you! Oh, you must be frozen solid! . . . ' Mrs. Garland hadn't changed either, her short grey-blonde hair framing the pleasant, readily-smiling face I remembered. She was huddled into various woollies topped by a lurid orange fleece, all finished off by oversized wellies. The outfit made her look as broad as she was long.

She gave me a warm welcoming hug. Always the two of us had got along.

'I'm fine,' I assured her. 'Have you heard again from Michelle?'

'She rang at lunchtime, Trev is still very poorly. Look, dear, let me show you your room first — you can be getting sorted while I make the tea, then we'll sit down and catch up on the news. — Oh, mind Tommy under your feet! I adopted him last week from the Catcarers people, he hasn't quite settled down yet.'

I didn't dare ask how many pets of her own complemented the array of boarders in the cabins outside.

There were sacks of *Pussynibbles* piled up in the hall, and a small mountain of *Tibbymeat* tins adorned by grinning feline faces. I followed Mrs. Garland upstairs to the landing and she pushed one of the cream-painted doors wider open. The bed by the window was occupied at present by an overweight ginger cat and a mangy-looking tiger-striped creature indulging in a detailed all-over scratch on the pillow. *My* pillow? . . .

'Shoo! — shoo! — Naughty boys!' Mrs. Garland clapped her hands at them mildly. 'Sorry about that, Bethany. I do hope you'll be comfortable here. The bathroom's next door — oh, Snowflake often sleeps in the bath so do check before you start running water!'

Past questioning anything, I promised to check.

While she vanished to the kitchen I carted my things upstairs. The house was gloomy on this miserable day, and the spare bedroom on the cramped side, especially for three. The thin striped cat, seeming to assess the situation, stalked off in disgust. The fat ginger one stayed put, green knowing eyes challenging me to try shifting him.

In ten minutes I was downstairs, more than ready for a hot drink. It was already steaming on a tray by a glowing gas fire, accompanied by scones and biscuits. Photos of past, present and maybe future cats adorned the mantelpiece. A calendar scrawled with notes hung above it.

Mrs. Garland explained, 'We eat about seven — not later, otherwise Grandpa gets indigestion and can't sleep. He has the front room as a bed-sit, I expect Michelle told you? — he was ill last year, it was time he moved in with us. Poor dear, he gets a bit muddled, and the animals do get on his nerves! — but at least we can keep an eye on him.'

I murmured assent, warming my hands on my mug. (It had a pattern of cats dancing with skipping-ropes around its base — what else would it have?)

'Michelle's been so good to me since her Daddy died,' my hostess rambled on. 'You know she gave up a nice job to help me get this place and run it, now she just does part-time reception at the vet's in the High Street. It's really given me something to live for, I do enjoy it! But of course, it's hard work. All the feeding and cleaning, you know, and we have extra pens for Catcarers, they bring us these poor sad moggies needing homes and send people to look at them. It's so rewarding when one of the cats gets a nice new home!'

'And if they don't get a home, you take them in yourself?'

'Sometimes!' she confessed. 'There's the paperwork too, and ordering in the supplies — all sorts of things, so I'm really grateful you've come to help. And I just don't know what I'll do if Michelle and Trev get married in September. That's what they planned before the accident. I suppose — ' She eyed me thoughtfully from her armchair. 'You wouldn't be interested in taking over from her here, would you?'

'Er — it's a bit early to know about September,' I said politely but in haste. I saw her gaze fix on my left hand, where two small, bright diamonds caught the light. 'I need to get a few things sorted with Toby. Our relationship is — well, a bit pear-shaped at present.'

'My dear, I'm so sorry. Michelle told me. Please don't think I'm prying, but — if it would help to talk about it? — '

'Maybe later,' I evaded. 'Thanks!'

On the mantelpiece a photo of Michelle and Trevor, their heads happily close, smiled down from among the cats. It brought a lump to my throat. They weren't smiling now. The lump came as well in remembering a similar photo of Toby and me marking our engagement, when all the world was bright.

It was a little over a year ago that I first met him: Toby Benjamin Gates, a couple of months younger, as fair as I was dark, as tall and well-built as I was short and slight and patron of 'petite' rails in fashion stores. I was running for a bus, and tripped over something and landed full tilt in his arms. We used to joke that he didn't 'sweep me off my feet' but back on to them. He saved me falling in the gutter. It was my heart that fell, and had never recovered.

The world took on a golden glow, during all that fleeting time when we were so much together, when those warm arms so often held me, when I lived for the smile in his blue eyes. Maybe I should have known a light so bright must sometime burn itself out?

It had faded already just a little when Toby had the chance to transfer for a spell to the French branch of the computer company where he worked. And he had jumped at the idea of Paris. There was some half-serious talk of me going with him: but at that time my father was undergoing an operation, and my parents needed my support.

So Toby went off alone. On the day he left, I even offered him back his ring. He seemed hurt and surprised, and for a while I was flooded with phone calls and postcards. But they, like that fairytale glow, had tailed off. Today, it seemed we were a world asunder.

The ring of the telephone was a welcome interruption to those memories.

'Probably Michelle — or it'll be Mrs. Joliffe asking after Bertie,' Mrs. Garland predicted as she jumped up. 'When she stays at her son's, she rings most days.'

It was indeed Bertie's owner. I heard her being assured the cat was eating well, and of course had a heater in his cabin.

This put an end to the fireside interlude. It was time for the boarders' evening feeds. I couldn't do less than offer to 'learn the ropes'.

They weren't too comfortable to learn, in the slushy, ear-nipping dusk. The previous time I visited here, in summery sunshine, the Cattery looked very pleasant with its rows of wooden chalets surrounding a patch of grass centred by bright flowers. Tonight, my feet were quickly awash and my fingers turned to icicles.

I had helped prepare the food bowls in an extension room built on to the kitchen. There were also water bowls and litter trays needing attention. The rescued cats were in a separate group of pens with attached exercise run, and these mournful creatures captured my instant sympathy: particularly a battered black and white cat missing half an ear.

'Poor old Alfie.' Mrs. Garland doled him out a helping of Pussynibbles. 'Who's going to want him when they can choose a pretty young one?'

Probably she was, I thought. My respect for her and her disordered dwelling had already grown.

Back indoors with a pile of unsavoury used bowls, she still had the evening meal to cook. She looked weary. I did the bowls in the sink in the extension room, and tried to clear the place up a bit, which it needed. Had Michelle been absent only two days? . . .

The meal was very well cooked, when at last it reached the table. Old Mr. Garland also arrived, a frail-looking gentleman with sparse white hair, bent shoulders and a rasping cough. He looked at me over his glasses in rather a puzzled way while we ate. Before the meal was finished, Michelle's call came through from Devon, first to talk to her mother, then to me.

'Bethany, you're a star. I can't tell you how grateful I am! We haven't even got Kathryn — the teenager who comes in odd hours to help — she's doing exams and her father put his foot down. And it's so much for Mum to handle, especially with Grandpa as well — '

'Please!' I cut her short. 'I'm here, and I'll do my best. It's a whole new way of life! Tell me about Trev, is he — ?'

Trevor wasn't good, she said. She evidently didn't want to go into details.

I promised her, 'We'll manage here, just don't worry about us. Trev needs you there with him.'

She sounded not far from tears. It made my own problems seem small.

By the time the meal was cleared away, and tomorrow's schedule checked (Mrs. Blake's Fluffy going out, one new boarder coming in) I was starting to feel as weary as Mrs. Garland looked. This stressful day was beginning to tell.

I was glad to get to my small room, ejecting Obese Ginger forcibly from my bed, and making very sure to turn over my pillow. Had I really supposed life at the Corner Cattery would be a sinecure?

* * *

It was around the very jolly hour of 3 a.m. when a commotion downstairs invaded my sleep. Blearily investigating, I found Grandpa had upset his bedside drink while seeking his lost spectacles to find an indigestion tablet. Mrs. Garland was trying to repair the damage, watched by a selection of cats.

'Did we wake you, dear? — I'm so sorry,' she apologised.

'It doesn't matter a bit. Can I help?'

I waded in to sort things out. While she warmed his hot water bottle I reassured his preliminary protests, 'Don't worry, Mr. Garland, I'm a nurse.' (I might as well use my universal passport!) I helped him get rid of the damp pyjamas and fixed up the bed. Either he stopped protesting or I just wasn't listening.

As I was leaving him, snugly tucked up again, surprisingly he called me back.

'Young lady! — whatever you're called, Grace told me some fancy name — '

'Bethany.'

'Bethany. Well, you've been very kind. Thank you!'

Which was encouraging. But huddling back in my bed, it seemed only an instant before my alarm shrilled me awake again. It was a gloomy, chilly morning.

Grandpa needed a breakfast tray in his room. The indoor cats needed feeding — especially Obese Ginger — and the outside boarders both their food and cleaning out. Our new arrival was due at 9 a.m.: also, a phone call from the Catcarers people announced that the Bradshaw family had passed their home check and would call on us later.

No time for twiddling thumbs, or dwelling too much on the journey to France that I wasn't making.

On the dot of nine a Miss Biddle arrived, with a basket containing — at first glance — just a huge mass of creamy-beige fur. Peering in more closely, I realised there were also a head and a tail, along with two short legs at each end. With the undoubtedly beauti-ful Persian came a daunting array of combs, brushes and special foods, and strict instructions from her owner.

'Princess must be groomed twice a day. Not just a quick flick, thoroughly. And it's essential she has her anti-hairball food.'

I assured her, only vaguely aware of what a 'hairball' might be, 'We're experienced with all breeds, Miss Biddle. Princess will be safe with us.'

'Well, I hope so.' The severe-faced lady handed over the cat's vaccination certificate dubiously. 'She won't be in any draughts? She won't mix with the rescued strays you keep here? — '

'Definitely not. Do feel free to ring us any time — but there's really no need.'

As Miss Biddle was bound for a stay in South Africa with a relative, hopefully she wouldn't ring too often. There again, she well might.

As she eventually left, she asked me again, 'You're positive you don't have any parasites? — fleas, lice, ticks? — '

Almost I answered, 'Not me personally.' Instead, I insisted gravely that all hygienic and medical standards were adhered to twenty-four-seven.

When the gate shut behind her, Mrs. Garland overwhelmed me with thanks.

'You're a godsend, Bethany! My dear, I really do hope you'll think about joining me here when — if — Michelle gets married? . . . '

I didn't have to answer that. Indeed, my 'godsend' status suddenly was in serious doubt. As we resumed our chores around the cabins, she gave a horrified gasp.

'Oh no! Oh, I don't believe this! — '

She was looking at the 'rescued' block. The door of the end cabin, labelled 'Granny', was partly open. The cabin was empty.

'But — but — ' I almost gabbled. 'I was doing that one when Miss Biddle came! A hoary-looking old thing missing a lot of fur?'

'Yes, that's Granny! Oh, she could be anywhere! — '

It was too late to realise what had happened — that the cabin door had an unreliable fastener, which was why a bolt had been added at the top of the

18

door: Mrs. Garland hadn't warned me, and the arrival of Princess had caused me to omit noticing it. And, my attention elsewhere, I hadn't secured the block's outer door. The damage was done. Granny, an unlikely fugitive, could well have taken her chance of the wide world when the gate was opened. She could even have stowed away in the basket Miss Biddle bore to her car, which really didn't bear considering.

'I'm so very sorry. It was my fault! But don't worry,' I encouraged Mrs. Garland, 'we'll find her. Let's check the house and garden first.'

A search of the whole premises proved sadly unproductive. Mrs. Garland shook her head hopelessly as we went out to the street and separated in opposite directions, both calling hopefully, both armed with mobile phones, cat-carriers and bags of Fishytreats.

It was a thoroughly miserable morning, the sky iron grey, a frosted slush underfoot. In fact, this seemed like a pleasant enough district whenever the front gardens would blossom at the touch of spring. At the moment spring was doing no touching at all.

'Granny, Granny? — nice Fishy-treats!' I called again, peering over gates, scanning roads and pavements — and aware how odd that invitation must sound. Not knowing the area, I ploughed on at random. A busier street surely would frighten the fugitive: might not this almost rural-looking backwater winding uphill, edged by only a few large old houses, be more likely?

I went slowly on my way, still calling and peering. The place was replete with trees, but could Granny conceivably climb a tree? Could she even have walked this far? The road was a cul-de-sac, and the very end house stood in a large spread of land, quite an imposing brick-built residence on three floors, graced by a Victorian-type conservatory at one side. Very nice, I thought in passing. I was actually turning away to try another direction when I spotted out of the corner of my eye a dark shape just squeezing beneath the gate, melting instantly away in that extensive garden.

This was no time for being polite and asking permission. I marched in and began searching. The garden sloped up some distance to the house, with terraced rockeries and rose-beds. Surely a black cat should show up obligingly against the snow, but this one didn't. I was still without sight nor sound of it when I was vaguely aware of being watched from the house. Shortly after, the front door opened.

What happened next, happened quickly. The cat broke cover and raced towards the house, at the same moment that a fair-haired man leaning on a walking stick came out with the clear intention of asking me what I was doing. My pursuit of the runaway was cut very short. The animal made a beeline for the open door — and tripped the man up on the slippery steps. To my horror, he fell heavily down the whole flight.

The horror was compounded by realisation that the cat, nipping smartly into the house, had one white foot and a white stomach, and probably lived here or nearby.

I stooped anxiously beside the man who had landed in a heap in the snow.

'Are you all right? — I'm terribly sorry about this! . . . look, don't try to move yet, just stay still. Do you have any pain anywhere? . . . '

The answer was sharp and unexpected.

'Everywhere. And I'm not a polar bear, so I'm going back inside.' He added, 'What were you doing in my garden?'

'I'm really sorry, I thought I saw Granny hiding in here — she's lost, you see. Come on, let me help you up!'

'Haven't you done enough damage already?' that sarcastic voice asked.

'Sorry! But you can trust me, I'm a nurse.' (This was getting monotonous?)

In fact, it wasn't at all easy to get him safely to his feet. He was maybe in his mid or late thirties, not particularly tall but powerfully built: there was a faint sprinkle of silver in his curly light-gold hair, contrasting with eyes as deep and moodily grey as this morning's sullen sky. It was obvious he had a disabled leg, necessitating the walking stick I retrieved for him. Despite grunts of protest, he did hang on to me quite hard up to the door.

'That fall must have shaken you up,' I said doubtfully. 'And you're shivering.'

'I've been lying in the snow. I'm entitled to shiver.'

I insisted, 'I feel responsible. At least let me just make sure you're comfortable? Please?'

We were inside the house now. I glimpsed a spacious hall floored with black and white tiles, a spiralling staircase, photographs and flowers. The room he grudgingly indicated was spacious too, its windows overlooking that fateful garden. There were sofas and deep chairs, glass-topped coffee tables, a distinctive old fireplace. In the

hearth a log-effect fire glowed cheer-
fully.

The chair closest to the fire con-
tained cushions and a plaid blanket. I
guessed it was from there he had
spotted me rooting around his garden.
Even when he regained the chair, and I
ignored impatient grunts to tuck the
blanket round him, I wasn't sure about
leaving him. No-one else in the big
house had materialised to investigate
our entrance.

'Are you alone here? Only I'm not
sure that's a good idea at the moment.'

'Mrs. Boyle is at the shops, my
mother is at the hairdressers. They'll
both be back shortly. Does that satisfy
you?' He added, 'Anyway, shouldn't
you be out looking for your Grandma
before the poor woman freezes to
death?'

I stared at him, and then realisation
dawned. 'Oh dear! No, you see, I was
looking for a lost cat . . . '

It would have been quite hilarious, if
I weren't still equally worried about the

missing animal and the accident on the steps. I started a confused explanation of who I was, where I was from, and why I was so blatantly trespassing. In the midst of it, my mobile phone jangled.

'Mrs. Garland, hello! Look, I'm really sorry, but — '

'It's all right, she's found!' Mrs. Garland fairly trilled the good news. 'She's on Grandpa's bed, he's shut her in and just rang to tell me!'

It was a big relief, not only for the cat's sake but it gave me time to linger here a while longer. I told Mrs. Garland, 'I'll be back soon, I'm just a bit tied up with something — I'll explain later.'

Whatever she imagined, she would scarcely picture me in the house of a taciturn and shivering stranger I had just dumped in the snow. Looking round at him I insisted, 'How about a hot drink to thaw you out? I think you should! Tea or coffee?'

He gave an exaggerated sigh. 'Coffee.

25

If you absolutely must. Black, no sugar. Very strong.'

His choice seemed to match his disposition — perhaps excusable just now. Leaving him by the fire I found a large and very well equipped kitchen, all gleaming units and cupboards, pale-rose tiles and shiny gadgets. From a stand of mugs I took one inscribed *The Boss*, which seemed appropriate.

While the water boiled, I could scarcely help viewing the messages on a big memo-calendar on the wall in front of me. Surprisingly, this seemed to be a busy family household: 'Dance rehearsals — new shoes for R?' and 'See Joe's teacher' and 'Cakes for School Fair' were just a few of them. Also, 'Ellen's birthday' and 'Hospital, Dr. Thorne'. On the table where doubtless pre-school breakfasts were gobbled were a pink hair-scrunchie and a few crayons. A discarded envelope from today's post was addressed 'Mr. Dominic Tremaine'.

Back in the other room, the accident

victim looked a trifle better. At least he was no longer shivering. The frown was unchanged.

I hadn't made myself a drink, and he didn't suggest I should. Standing there like a spare part while he sipped his sinister brew, I found myself facing an attractive portrait photo on the mantelpiece of a young boy and a younger girl. I commented, 'That's a nice picture! No mistaking he's your son!'

'As a matter of fact, they're not my children.'

'They're not? That's amazing, he looks just like you.'

'I'm their uncle. They live here just at present. They're called Joe and Rhiannon, if you're so interested.'

'Rhiannon? That's an unusual name.'

'Their mother was Welsh — if you're desperate to know that too.'

It wasn't the easiest of conversations. But maybe his brand of heavy sarcasm showed he was feeling better. I was just thinking it was time to leave him to stew in his own acerbic juice when a large silver car swooped into the snowy drive just outside the window. Its occupant got out, and a key turned in the front door.

Advancing into the hall to explain myself, I faced a tall, vaguely condescending lady with arched eyebrows, upswept blonde-tinted hair and undeniably a very stylish get-up even on this wintry day. 'Mother from the hairdressers', I guessed, not 'Mrs. Boyle from the shops'?

She stared at me, with the unexpected question, 'You're not the press, are you?'

'No!' I assured her. 'I'm the cat boarding-house down the road. Bethany Brown. There was just — er a little accident on the steps, I came in to try to help — '

'Dominic? Is he all right? — ' She pushed past me without waiting for an answer. 'Nicci, darling, what happened? — whatever were you doing outside, didn't I warn you not to go out? — shall I phone the doctor? — '

'I'm all in one piece. Will you please not fuss?'

As she bent anxiously over his chair, I decided it was definitely time to leave. I coughed in the background and announced, 'I'll be going now, and I'm so sorry for all the problems.'

She answered with the merest nod. My erstwhile patient looked at me across the room — and said surprisingly, 'Good luck with the cats. And thanks for the coffee and TLC, matron.'

With the words went the first glimmer of a smile I had seen, strangely transforming that moodily serious face.

I gathered up the bits and pieces abandoned in the garden and plodded my way back to the Corner Cattery. Mrs. Garland, just finishing off at the cabins, looked exhausted.

'Go inside, I'll do this,' I said. 'Then we'll both have a nervous breakdown together, Mrs. Garland!'

'Oh, my dear, please do make it 'Grace' . . . It really was a morning, wasn't it?'

'It was! I wonder — do you know anything about the big house at the end of Bramble Hill? A man called — Dominic Something?'

'Oh yes, he's our local celebrity! Dominic Tremaine, the playwright! You must have heard of him — he's just had another big success in London. But he's quite a recluse. No-one ever sees him.'

'I saw him! I made him some very black coffee. He seemed sort of sad for a successful man . . . '

She didn't hear, already on her way to the house. I set to work on the last of our belated chores. Finally, aware of a reinstated Granny giving me a bleary glance, for some reason I ladled into her dish an extra portion of Fishytreats.

★   ★   ★

The Bradshaw family arrived about four, and there was an excited debate about choosing a pet. Neither Granny nor Alfie got a look-in. For some strange reason, I was quite glad. The family left with a pretty young tabby called Stripey.

I persuaded Mrs. Garland to lie down for a snooze. Taking her father a cup of tea in his room, where he was poring over his stamp collection, I told him, 'Grandpa, you're the hero of the hour!' He hadn't got hold of my name yet, but I was rewarded by a crusty smile. Maybe it might be helpful to involve him a little more in the backroom Cattery work, to make him feel part of the team?

The evening meal again was interrupted by Michelle's call. The news was no better. When I helped presently with the washing-up, I saw her mother wasn't far from tears.

'Grace, he's stable, he's young and strong,' I whispered.

'I — I know . . . but he and Michelle had so many plans . . . they were such a lovely couple . . . '

'They still are. And the plans might need adapting, but they're still there.'

Instinctively, I opened my arms to

her and for a moment held her close.

'I'm so sorry, Bethany, it's just — ' Suddenly she was sobbing. 'I just wish I had my Frank here to help us get through this . . . '

Her husband had died very suddenly barely three years ago. All this grave talk of hospitals of course had brought her own loss flooding back. I stayed with her till she was calmer. There were times when a qualified nurse wasn't needed, just a fellow human-being.

With the chores done, a frost crisping up the slushy snow and nipping my feet that had already got wet more than once, I was ready to call this peculiar day closed. Princess hadn't been groomed, hissing spitefully at us from the back of her pen. A nice little job for someone tomorrow.

Before settling down to sleep I thought, as I always thought, of phoning Toby. Would it do any good? Mostly it meant leaving a message. He must by now have had the letter I sent last week. His most recent communication was a pretty postcard that said nothing at all.

I looked at the photograph propped up on my dressing-table of the two of us, taken on the boating holiday we had early last summer — it seemed a century ago: Toby standing tall and straight beside the little motor-launch we hired, the sparkle on the water matching the radiance of his laughter, that errant strand of golden-brown hair flopped across his forehead. Beside him, in rather ridiculously nautical tee-shirt and cropped jeans, short and dark and sun-tanned, I was laughing too as though there were no tomorrows.

No tomorrows. Please heaven, there would be for Michelle and Trevor, at least for them. On an impulse I snatched up the photo and interred it in a drawer under a wad of jumpers.

Another day did dawn, before I was really ready for it. During breakfast there arrived too one of Toby's cheery text messages:

'HI, THANX 4 NICE LETTR, SPEAK 2U SOON. XXX.'

'There, you see!' Grace encouraged with kind anxiety. 'The poor boy's probably just very busy.'

Busy with just what? Toby was never, never, a workaholic.

Mona Halstead from Catcarers had told us we would be receiving a replacement for Stripey. Hosing down the cabin in readiness, I managed to hose my feet as well — and attempting to use Michelle's wellingtons, much too large, almost tripped me up. I decided, 'Grace, I've got to get some boots! Where should I go?'

She told me a bus from down the road to Croydon town centre was the best bet, saving the hassle of parking. I waited till the afternoon so I could meet Mona: a plump, cheery, kind-faced lady, who warmed my heart a little by telling me, 'Lovely to have you on board, dear!' It was as well she didn't know about Granny.

A clock was chiming quarter-past three when I arrived amid the big, busy town's plethora of fashionable stores and giant office-blocks, eateries and bars, pedestrian walkways and gliding tramcars. It took a while to search out what I needed. Even then, the rubber boots were lurid pink patterned with white daisies. No matter, they might brighten up our inmates.

I bought some other odds and ends. After that, there was just time for a quick cuppa before returning to the fairly chaotic bus station. In one of those numerous cafes, with many tables grouped outside in a glass-roofed walkway, I paid for a mug of tea and a blueberry muffin, and was just making for a seat when a sudden realisation diverted me in a different direction.

'Hello again!' I greeted the man occupying a table with two schoolchildren, a light-haired boy and a dark, pretty-faced young girl. 'I'm so glad you've recovered from the accident yesterday, it's a weight off my mind!'

'Sorry? Yesterday — ?'

For a moment I just stared, wondering if he had hit his head hard when he fell on the steps. He was looking at me as though he had never seen me before. Then there followed a somewhat wry smile.

'I'm afraid you've made the usual mistake. I'm not Dominic Tremaine.'

'But — you must be!' Already hampered by carrier-bags, I almost dropped my tray. 'You're exactly the same! *Exactly* the same!'

'I know. We're twins.' The smile had deepened. 'The identical sort. It causes a lot of confusion. Look, why not sit down before you collapse?'

He had jumped up to help me. I mumbled dazed thanks while accepting the fourth chair at the table.

'Well, I — I'm sorry to barge in! — but I really did think — '

'Don't worry, it often happens,' he reassured me. 'People do find it unnerving.'

I was noticing now one or two subtle

points. He was drinking undeniably white coffee. In his curly fair hair there was no noticeable encroachment of grey. Especially, there was no walking stick propped up by his chair.

'Mum rang me last night about Dominic having a fall,' he was going on. 'She said it was because some idiot girl was looking for a lost cat.'

'Yes, the idiot girl was me! Bethany Brown, from the Corner Cattery — I let the silly thing escape on my first day working there — '

'Too bad,' he sympathised.

'Wasn't it just? I'm just helping out temporarily, I'm on leave from nursing — which is why I tried to do my best to help your brother, I felt awful about it!'

'Nicci isn't good at being helped, is he?'

'I discovered that,' I agreed. I took a gulp of the cooling tea that hadn't been slopped out of the mug. 'And I'm afraid I really must rush off now for a bus . . . '

He followed up my self-introduction.

'I'm Doctor Tremaine if we're being formal — Darryl if we're not! . . . Listen, don't rush for buses, the queues are hell at this time of day! I have to drop these two off at their Grandma's in Bramble Hill, so why don't I drop you off too? Sit still and recover, I'll just get you another tea — Rhiannon, no, you aren't having more ice-cream! Joe, will you sit up and take your elbows off the table? . . . '

Darryl Tremaine's eyes were the same deep, dark grey as his brother's, but you wouldn't call it storm-grey. His smile had warmth and humour and kindness.

I mumbled, 'It's really very kind of you.'

I took a large bite of my blueberry muffin.

2

Grace Garland shook her head at the sight of me emerging from a total stranger's car with my bags and bundles. But chiefly she was still glowing after an excited call from Michelle a few minutes ago. Trevor was a shade better, he had spoken a few words.

We shared our delight. It was too soon to count chickens, but until now all the news had been gloom and doom.

In a while, I got round to explaining the happenings of the afternoon, and my conversation with Darryl Tremaine during the ride home. A surprisingly free and easy chat, it had proved to be. He thanked me for taking care of his brother. I learnt that he was himself largely working abroad for a medical charity, which was the reason his motherless children stayed mostly with their Grandmother at Bramble Hill.

'She's so good with them, it works very well. At least, it does when Nic is living at his other address — ' He pulled himself up abruptly. 'That's another story! Mustn't wash the family's dirty linen in public.'

He was here in England for a spell, and today had met the children from school to shop for new shoes. He was genuinely interested to know I was nursing at Mid-Counties Park, asking a string of questions about my work there.

All the way home, neither of the children had much to say. Rhiannon grumbled at getting boring school shoes instead of something pretty. It was the sight of the Corner Cattery notice that suddenly awoke Joe: he enquired how many cats we had, what food we gave them, did they get any exercise — and could he come in to look them over personally.

His father apologised, 'This isn't really a grilling from an animal health inspectorate! It's just his big ambition is to be a vet, you see. I keep telling him, at present he needs to concentrate hard on his schoolwork.'

'But it's a splendid ambition. You stick with it, Joe,' I encouraged the boy. 'And I'll talk to the owner, I'm sure she'll let you look round one day. I'll drop by and let you know, you're only five minutes away.'

I wasn't sure why I said that, instead of asking Grace here and now, or even more reasonably asking for the Bramble Hill phone number.

Grace didn't know either, commenting it was strange how I was getting so involved with the entire Tremaine family. She laughed, in her new relief at Michelle's news, 'Who knows, maybe Dominic Tremaine will give out free tickets for one of his plays!'

'I can't see him giving out anything,' I admitted. 'Unless it's a 'No Trespassing' notice.'

I took over the evening chores so Grace could cook a meal in peace. Our new arrivals, tabby sisters called, for some reason, Itzy and Bitzy, were sharing the big end cabin, looking a little bewildered. I made an extra fuss of them. Princess turned her aloof back on me. But I also found myself chatting companionably to some of the residents: 'How are you tonight, Bertie?' and 'Nice din-dins, Montmorency!' — and 'Granny, will you stop glaring at my pink boots? . . . '

Toby would warn darkly, 'Another week here, Beth, and they'll be sending for the green van.' Toby would say all kinds of teasing things. Probably he still was . . . but exactly who was listening to them?

It seemed Grace was quite happy for Joe Tremaine to see round the Cattery, but it couldn't happen the next day, Saturday: for we woke to find a cardboard box of kittens dumped by our gate — four thin, wailing, shivering scraps of soiled fur.

An SOS brought Mona along in her van. I watched with respect as she

42

calmed and comforted the forlorn little creatures, and then went with her to the local veterinary surgery. Afterwards she took the kittens off to the Main Shelter — 'Rest and rehab,' she explained to me, 'but hopefully you'll get a couple back for rehoming.'

I said, 'They deserve to go somewhere very nice!'

'A shame you haven't found any takers for Granny. I was wondering about transferring her to one of our other places — '

'Oh, I'm sure she'll strike lucky with us soon!' I broke in.

She invited me to visit the Main Shelter one day. All the while it kept crossing my mind how interested Joe would be in all this. Maybe, if his family agreed, I could take him with me when that visit happened.

The stressful Saturday went on as it began, with Miss Biddle phoning about Princess, and someone wanting to assess our accommodation, and someone else enquiring if we would accept a diabetic cat as an emergency. I heard Grace telling her, 'No problem at all, my colleague here is an experienced nurse.'

Her faith in my abilities was flattering, if somewhat alarming.

With the morning jobs done, plus a review of the recent paperwork, after lunch I seized a chance to slip out for a couple of hours. My footsteps carried me unerringly to Bramble Hill. Today, with no preliminary rooting in the garden, I rang the bell.

It was a spare, severe-faced woman in a nylon overall who opened the door and greeted me dourly, 'If you're the press, everyone's out!'

Were these people paranoid about the press?

'I'm not,' I assured her. 'I've come to see Joe, Dr. Tremaine knows all about it.'

'Dr. Tremaine isn't here till later.' Her narrow dark eyes surveyed me suspiciously. 'You'd better call back in an hour.'

'That's not convenient. Can't I leave a message?'

'That depends,' she said unhelpfully.

'Just a simple message. Is that really too much to ask? — '

I was starting to get annoyed. But we were interrupted by another voice asking, or demanding, 'What's the problem here?'

She said in her sharp way, 'I'm sorry, Mr. Tremaine, but this young lady — '

'This young lady is a friend of mine. You can leave us to sort it out, thank you.'

'If you say so! I do *try* to follow Mrs. Tremaine's instructions.'

As she melted away with obvious reluctance, I was left facing my erstwhile patient. Leaning on his silver-mounted stick, he favoured me with a nod.

'Good afternoon, matron. Did you lose Granny again? — or just wonder if I survived your last visit?'

'Well — neither, really. I came to tell Joe he can visit the Cattery to see the animals.'

'He's out just now. They all went to the Park — but they won't be long. Do you want to wait inside?'

'Please,' I agreed readily. 'If it's no trouble.'

For the second time I stepped into that spacious hallway. Today, in less stressful circumstances, I took in more of the surroundings: especially a group of framed theatre bills and programmes mounted in an alcove, several featuring a play titled 'The Second Bed From The Window'. A few of the posters displayed extracts from press reviews: *'This one will have you in tears . . . '* and *'This sensitive saga of family life is unmissable . . . '* and *'Dominic Tremaine's beautifully crafted drama deserves all its high acclaim . . . '*

'This way,' I was invited. He lowered his voice. 'My sanctum — the only privacy in the house. Out of bounds to the aproned ogress.'

Following his laboured steps, I couldn't suppress a schoolgirl giggle.

He unlocked a door at the back of

the house. The agreeably cluttered room was obviously a sort of workroom-cum-den: its wide windows looked out on the spread of rear garden, lawns and flower-beds and at one side children's swings. There was a well-worn sofa by the fire, an old-fashioned writing desk scattered with papers, shelf upon shelf of books in higgledy-piggledy rows and piles. Two or three emptied coffee mugs sat unhygienically around. More books and papers oozed from a wooden filing cabinet, and more or less everywhere else.

He asked, as I gazed about in fascination, 'Can you imagine what Mrs. Boyle would do with this if ever she got in here?'

'She'd vacuum your carpet, for a start!'

'I can live with the dust. I can't live with interference.'

'And can you always find what you need?' I suggested.

'Eventually. At least the search is interesting. Will you sit down, Miss

— oh, wasn't it 'Bethany'?'

'It was. It still is!'

'I'm Dominic. As you probably know.'

Those dark grey eyes of his were certainly less like storm clouds than on our last meeting. But the stifled grunt he gave as he sat down by the desk made me ask contritely, 'I'm sorry, I should have asked — I hope you didn't have too many after-effects from the other day?'

'Some picturesque bruises. Which I don't propose to show you. No, this is a very long-standing problem.'

'An accident?' I hazarded.

'Well. Let's say, a sort of accident.'

To my prosaic way of thinking, either an accident was an accident or it wasn't. I could scarcely ask for a case history.

It was hard to believe this conversation at all — and it still went on while I sat there on his somewhat sagging sofa. He asked why I was boarding cats instead of nursing people, and I explained about that, the tiny flat I shared with a fellow nurse just outside Leicester, the SOS from Michelle that had brought me here. I didn't mention Toby: I wasn't wearing my engagement ring, which was sharing a drawer with Toby's photo. (After all, it could so easily be damaged working in the cat cabins? . . .)

In turn, I learnt that Joe and Rhiannon's mother, Glynis Tremaine, had died when Rhiannon was still a baby, and their Grandmother had very competently taken them over. 'Because Darryl spends most of his time in Africa,' Dominic said; noticeably the only mention of his twin brother, hardening his face and his voice. He added that Rhiannon was blatantly spoiled. Joe was Trouble.

Most amazing of all, when I ventured to ask what he was currently working on, he indicated a thick mass of scribbled A4 on the desk. I marvelled, 'All handwritten! — you don't have a computer?'

'The boy has one upstairs. I hate the things! — totally inhuman. With pen and paper you can live what you're writing. I've a good typist — a funny old girl but excellent at her job, she makes sense of it when it reaches that stage.' He added with a frown, 'She should have typed it long ago, it's way overdue. I just can't finish the damn thing off.'

'Oh dear. Is it meant to have a happy ending?'

He said quietly, 'Is there such a thing as a happy ending?' I followed his gaze to the windowsill where one flowering plant stood, an orchid exquisite in its exotic beauty. 'The play is called *Pale Orchid*, it's a love story. The orchid flowers in a glory of white purity, the blooms endure so long you think they'll be here for always — but their turn will come to wither and die.'

I nodded. The words struck home, suddenly robbing me of my voice, filling my eyes with tears. I realised he was looking with concern into my face.

'Forgive me, Bethany. Did I say something wrong?'

Was it foolish imagination that he said my name like no-one else said it? I managed to whisper, 'No, not wrong at all. It — it's true, what you said.'

'You've found that out, then? Me too.' He turned abruptly back to the desk. 'I've been working on this nearly a couple of years, and I'm struggling. And I get these annoying diversions — like next week I'm giving a sort of lecture at the LLDF. The London Literature and Drama Foundation. I can't think why I agreed to do it! . . . '

LLDF. Very carefully I filed the name away in my memory.

It was the sound of a key in the front door and intrusive voices that ended that strangely intimate interlude. I pulled myself together to say a stilted 'Hello!' to Mrs. Tremaine, she of the supercilious eyebrows, and returned Darryl Tremaine's friendly nod. Rhiannon had obviously been crying, and stormed straight upstairs. Joe had his sulky face on while his Grandmother berated him sharply for treading dirt into the house. (I looked hastily at my own feet.) He gave just a disappointing non-committal grunt when I delivered my Cattery invitation.

'That's kind of you, Miss — er — ' Mrs. Tremaine had a way of looking you up and down as though pricing every item of clothing you wore. 'If you're sure you want this young scamp creating mayhem around the place.'

I felt Joe wasn't really a 'scamp'. He seemed to me far more a troubled child with a sadly unsettled background.

Dominic hadn't reappeared, and Darryl vanished upstairs in the wake of Rhiannon. There seemed no reason to prolong my stay. Mrs. Tremaine saw me off the premises with a remote 'Good afternoon.' Then she added, as though unable to contain the question, 'Er — did I see you coming out of Dominic's study?'

'That's right. He was showing me his work.'

She gazed at me as though doubting her ears, and I elaborated, 'Yes, all handwritten because computers have no soul!'

'Well. That's quite extraordinary.' Her eyebrows had virtually vanished into her hair. 'No-one is allowed in there. No-one is ever allowed to see what he's writing.'

Her attitude indicated that I had committed some dastardly crime. I didn't much care.

Back along the chilly roads, I still repeated to myself like a mantra, 'L-L-D-F.' They must surely be in the phone book?

★   ★   ★

They were in the phone book. The lecture session, I was told, was on Wednesday evening.

Meantime, our immediate problem was the diabetic cat, brought in by its worried owner. Mrs. Croft, a small, pale woman, was entering hospital for an

53

operation but obviously was far more anxious for the docile sober-grey cat. She handed me his insulin supplies and a whole page of instructions in shaky handwriting.

'Only, you see, I've never left him before,' she apologised miserably.

'Smokey will be fine. I'll look after his treatment very carefully,' I promised.

There were tears brimming in her eyes as I showed her out, and they were tugging at mine too. It seemed some mixed-up emotions were very near the surface just now.

As well as Smokey, we had another arrival that day. Grace took a phone message and hurried outside to tell me about it.

'From Dr. Tremaine, he said was it all right to bring his boy along after school — and I said it was. He sounds nice!'

'He's very nice,' I agreed.

She was quite excited about receiving the family of 'a famous writer', she said reverently. I warned her still not to expect any free theatre tickets.

Darryl arrived about four with Joe in tow. The boy looked neat and tidy in his school uniform, and I was pleased that the usual attitude of insolent sulkiness quickly gave way to absorbed interest as I led him around and answered his questions. They were intelligent questions. My brief experience was quite sorely stretched.

He was especially interested in the exotic Princess, she of the prolific fur and pugnacious claws, and in the dreaded furballs.

'It hasn't happened yet, she's keeping us in suspense,' I told him. 'And this poor little fellow is Smokey, he's diabetic. Do you know what that means?'

'You give him insulin. I know all about that. They thought Rhiannon had it, but it was something else — she keeps seeing Dr. Thorne at the hospital.'

'Does she, Joe? I hope it's not anything bad.'

He shrugged. 'She's better since Christmas. But she told me, if she cries and makes a big fuss, Grandma gives her lots of treats. Two new dolls and a pram the other day, and a new bike — birthday presents, Grandma said. Bet you she'll get a load more before then.'

I murmured a thoughtful 'Ah!'

There was no chance to delve deeper, as his father and Grace were coming out from the house, and Grace announced tea was waiting. 'And whatever you'd like, Joe,' she told him kindly. 'Did you enjoy seeing the animals, dear?'

'They're great. It's nice here! Couldn't I — ?' He paused, and then plunged. 'If I could come and help here after school, I'd still have time for homework. I could help with cleaning up, I'd do anything — even the yucky things! — '

Darryl said with his pleasant laugh, 'Don't make any commitments you'll regret, Mrs. Garland!'

She seemed rather bereft of words. I

suggested, 'It's possible — just now and then — you could wash some plates, fill water bowls, Joe. How about that?'

'Anything!' he repeated earnestly.

As we trailed inside to the warmth of the house, he would plainly rather have stayed outside. I saw his pitying gaze linger on our 'Rescued' block, and whispered, 'I'll fix it for you! — I think you have a real affinity for the animals.'

He asked suspiciously, 'What's that?' I put a reassuring hand on his shoulder, and he didn't shake it off.

A tea-tray was waiting, and cakes and biscuits set out on Grace's best china. But Joe's interest was quickly diverted by discovering the in-house pets. He followed Obese Ginger and Skinny Tabby upstairs — and in his absence, Darryl related a couple of enlightening stories.

'When he was quite small — just before Rhiannon was born — one chilly day his Mum was visiting her friend, who had an old cat that was trying to get nearer the fire. Benji knocked down the guard, and — well, his tail started smouldering. Quite nasty! Joe was alone with him. He smothered the problem with a cushion, and then marched out to the kitchen to tell them, 'Benji caught fire. I've put it out, but you'd better look at him.' '

Grace marvelled, 'And how old was the little lad?'

'About two and a half. Another time — much more recently — he discovered two severed parts of a worm in the garden after his Grandma's gardener had been working. I found it later in the greenhouse, supplied with a tray of earth and leaves — and sellotaped together.'

'Bless his heart! One day you'll be very proud of him, Dr. Tremaine!'

'Let's hope so. Unfortunately, there's a downside. His behaviour at home and at school is — shall we say, interesting? I don't want that happening here, so I'm not sure if — '

'I don't think we'll have any problems with him!' I broke in quite rudely.

He looked at me with still that pleasant, friendly smile. 'But do be warned. Don't judge by today.'

'We want to encourage him. If he could be dropped off just once or twice a week, I'll see him home personally.'

It appeared the matter was settled. Joe's father seemed surprised by my insistence, but he raised no more objections.

But before he left, Darryl talked to us about his work in Africa, helping remote villages ravaged by drought and disease. His descriptions were graphic and moving. All three of us — including Grandpa, dunking biscuits in his tea in the background — were deeply interested.

Finally, Joe was rounded up from my bedroom where he was stroking Obese Ginger on the bed. The boy's too moody face (as moody as his Uncle Dominic's?) lit up at the news that he could help out at the Cattery.

A bleak and chilly evening had settled down outside when Grace and I saw the visitors off. She waved them a warm farewell. It had been arranged that Darryl would bring Joe after school on Friday — a day not clashing with football practice and trips to Rhiannon's dancing classes. He told me, 'See you then, Bethany, and on your own head be it!'

There was no way you could avoid smiling back when he smiled at you.

We were scarcely indoors before Grace enthused, 'What a very nice man! And — do you know — I was watching him, and he's really taken with you, dear! Had you noticed?'

I said non-committedly, 'Maybe. But he does have big problems with his family, more than he realises. One gets all the treats, one gets all the blame. And he's not around to sort it out.'

I wondered, how exactly did the balance lie between Dr. Tremaine's skilled and much needed work overseas, and the care of his own children? Was it right to live his life so far away from his ailing daughter and his troubled son?

— and should someone point it out to him? And, was any of it remotely my business? . . .

They were urgent, largely unanswerable questions.

'Come on, Grace,' I rallied her, 'you do the chores in here, I'll do the feeds. And one of us must comb that little witch Princess again before she gets mistaken for an unmade bed . . . '

* * *

Friday was yet to come. First there was Wednesday, bringing the fairly disgusting gift of a furball from Princess. Though ridding herself of it must have caused the poor creature discomfort, she eyed me quite gleefully when I arrived to clean her cabin.

As always, I paused an extra moment beside Granny to murmur some kind words and gently scratch her threadbare ears.

Chiefly, of course, Wednesday was the date for Dominic's London lecture.

Grace pooh-poohed my doubts about leaving her alone: I was here as a favour, I was worth my weight in gold, and I must go out whenever I wanted! In fact, with much more upbeat bulletins from Michelle, and the diversion of her awed interest in the Tremaines, she looked much brighter than when I joined her a few days ago.

I was catching the 6.32 train. Well before that, I prepared the evening feeds. At the last minute I changed into a dark trouser-suit, purchased in the Winter Sales, which was smart and fashionable and worn only twice. With it went a leaf-green shirt that seemed to bring out the hint of auburn in my dark hair. Toby used to say, wearing green turned my eyes from hazel to emerald. Toby used to say so many things like that.

Grace approved, 'You look nice! I expect Dr. Tremaine will be there to hear his brother, won't he? — maybe you can sit with him? . . . Have a good time, don't hurry back!'

The snow had left us, but it was a bleak enough evening with a hint of chill drizzle. The 6.32, of course, was delayed: 'A signal failure', the metallic loudspeaker voice apologised. When the train did appear, it dawdled all the way. I would need a miracle to reach the hall on time.

The busy terminus was awash with business commuters trying to cope with other delays, milling around the notice-boards. Outside, I joined a lengthy bus queue. I was shivering, because the smart suit wasn't particularly warm.

Finally scrambling on a bus, I wasn't sure of the area and got off too soon, entailing a hurried walk along damply glistening pavements, with a tide of traffic sweeping past. But at last, here was the weathered old building of St. Mordaunt's College, and across a paved courtyard the hall entrance: a notice by the door announced, 'The London Literature & Drama Foundation — To-night, *Modern Drama Debated:* with

Special Guest Speaker, Dominic Tremaine.'

The proceedings were already more than ten minutes old. The lady on the door whispered, 'Not much room left — you'll find a single right in front on the left.' So much for slipping unobtrusively into the back row.

And as if it weren't conspicuous enough to walk the length of the hall, I dropped my handbag as I sat down in the very front, and several loose coins and a comb and lipstick rolled out.

'Sorry!' I muttered. The tall silver-haired man speaking on the platform paused and cleared his throat.

Three other people were sitting at a table beside him, with notes and tumblers of water: a keen-looking man with dark-rimmed glasses, a woman of mature years whose face was vaguely familiar, and Dominic. He sat at the end, his walking stick propped against his chair. His hair was golden-blond under the light. His face expressed, more than anything, sheer boredom.

But he had noticed me. (How could anyone present *not* notice me?) And deliberately, as he met my eyes, he winked. I winked back.

The two supporting speakers — Don Someone who was a theatre critic for a magazine, Letitia Frayne a former stage actress — could have spoken Outer-Mongolian or Martian for all the sense they made to me. After them, the silver-haired LLDF Chairman introduced his star guest: 'Ladies and gentlemen, we're privileged to have with us a writer of international acclaim, author of several popular and thought-provoking plays — especially 'The Second Bed From The Window' and his current success 'The Answer' . . . Please welcome Dominic Tremaine, who will talk to us about his work. Then we'll take your questions.'

Why was my heart pounding against my ribs in this crazy fashion? Dominic looked as cool as an iced cucumber as he began with a wry apology: 'Forgive me for not getting up to talk to you . . . '

The comment made the other speakers, who had all stood at the lectern, look as though they wished they hadn't. Typical Dominic, I thought, this half-serious bitterness. Which posed another impossible question, how did I know that when really I knew him so little? . . .

His talk wasn't long, but it was fascinating, covering plotting and construction, dialogue and characterisation. Afterwards he answered effectively numerous questions from the audience. When the silver-haired man rose at last to call a halt and thank the speakers, there was prolonged applause.

As the proceedings broke up, Dominic beckoned to me. I went uncertainly near to the platform.

'Good evening, matron. Isn't this rather outside your sphere?'

'No, I do like the theatre. So — '

He looked at me in obvious disbelief. 'So why not go there tonight instead of sitting through this talking-shop? I've a hired car picking me up, would you like a ride home?'

The offer was so utterly unexpected that I just stared and mumbled. He seemed to take that as a 'Yes,' turning to speak to Letitia Frayne.

My immediate reactions were again nothing short of crazy. First, to find a cloakroom to see if I looked more presentable than I felt. Second, an urge just to jump happily up and down — which would have created a stir in the emptying hall. In fact, there was no time for either. Almost at once I was being escorted with Dominic via a back entrance to a private parking area.

A sleek black car was waiting, and the chauffeur opened the doors for us. I resisted a strong urge to help Dominic in, again instinctively knowing his reaction. The man from the Drama Foundation, who had shown us out, shook hands with him and quite warmly with me too, seeming to consider us an established 'item'. That didn't seem to bother Dominic, so why should it bother me?

Item or no, it was certainly preferable to glide into the stream of traffic in this classy limo instead of joining a queue for a bus to the station.

'It's really kind of you! — I had a ghastly time getting here, the trains were all haywire.' I felt I was babbling foolishly. 'That's why I was late, I felt awful about that! — '

'And was the occasion worth all the trouble?'

'Of course. Really interesting!'

'Was it? Blackbourne talks the same sort of piffle as he writes. Poor dear Letitia is getting past it.'

'Well, your part was worth it!' I insisted. 'But you left something out, you know.'

For the first time his bored sarcasm gave way to interest.

'What did I leave out?'

'That a computer doesn't have a soul.'

'Oh. You remembered that.' For the

first time too I saw him laugh, his too sombre face becoming suddenly and startlingly younger.

I remembered. Every word he had said to me, kind or unkind, I remembered. I chattered on, 'And you didn't talk about the play you're working on, did you?'

'Certainly not. I never do that, not to anyone.'

'But you talked about it to me,' I said simply.

Again there was that reaction of surprise. He said, 'So I did.'

The dark streets were slipping by much too fast. Every traffic light shone infuriatingly green. Along the way he grumbled some more about the theatre critic. He asked me how much longer I was staying with my friends — which I couldn't really answer. Everything was so indefinite. And there was still, of course, Paris and Toby? . . .

'I'll be around a while yet,' was the best I could do. 'And I might see you, because Joe wants to help at the Cattery and I'll be bringing him home. We've had an OK from your brother — you probably know about it?'

'If it concerns my brother, I probably don't.'

I muttered, 'Oh.' In the glare of shop lights we were passing, I saw his face was again cold and stern.

So very soon we reached the Cattery, where lights shone in the house. It amused me to think of Grace's reactions if she saw me a second time leaving a second man's car!

'Thanks again for the lift.' The chauffeur had jumped out to open my door, and I stood on the kerb feeling like Lady Muck in my Winter Sales 30%-Off suit.

'My great pleasure. By the way, there's a 'Save Our Local Theatre' meeting in a few days — the Council want to bulldoze it, I'm supposed to be on the platform to whip up a public protest. Maybe you'd fancy filling up a seat and applauding in the right places? I'll let you know the details. Goodnight,

Bethany. Sleep well.'

'I'm sure I shall — if I can manage to eject Obese Ginger from my bed.'

'*Who?*' The startled expression this time was quite comical.

'Just one of our cats. Goodnight, Mr . . . Night-night, Dominic, see you around!'

He was laughing as the car drove away. I carried that precious laughter with me up to the house. It was extraordinary that a radiant sun seemed to be shining through the bleak darkness. It was even stranger that someone's bleeping car-alarm sounded like the sweetest melody of a nightin-gale.

3

'Joe, we'll need a couple more tins of food. And this is Princess' special diet, we mustn't get that wrong!' Grace seemed quite impressed with her new helper. 'And this is for Smokey, he has a diet too.'

'He's the diabetic one, right? Has he had his insulin?'

'He has it in the mornings,' she confirmed.

It was Joe's first session at the Cattery, and we were doing the evening feeds. Darryl had dropped him off after school: the tall, fair-haired boy arrived in businesslike jeans and sweatshirt, even with his own protective gloves — and enough enthusiasm to run a multi-acre farm.

'You're a quick learner! I'm sure you're doing well at school, dear,' Grace added with kind but unfortunate interest. Joe's face quickly darkened.

'No. I got sent to Old Beaky today again. Just for punching Conor Reeves.'

I asked reasonably, 'Why did you punch Conor Reeves?'

'He was trying to scoop an alive snail out of its shell. He swore he never did and Old Beaky believed him and he's sending a note to Grandma. Again.' He shrugged his shoulders. 'Can we feed the cats now?'

'We can,' I agreed, and had to add, ' 'Old Beaky'?'

'Mr. Bilson. His nose looks like a beak.'

I muttered, 'Ah!' Life with our new 'Animal Welfare Assistant', as I had grandly titled him, looked like being interesting.

In fact, we did get the work done more quickly. By the time Darryl arrived back — on this first trial evening he was collecting as well as delivering — Grace had already laid out teacups, biscuits and home-baked cakes. Her 'best china' was having a

73

busy time of late.

Surprisingly, Joe had been drawn into Grandpa's room, after gravely greeting the old man, 'Hi, I hope you're well today?' A peep round the door showed the white head and the fair bent over one of the big stamp albums.

Darryl was asking with apprehension, 'How did it go? Don't spare me!'

'No need to spare you. It was fine,' I said.

Grace elaborated, 'We enjoyed having him! Bring him any time!'

He made a gesture of wiping his brow in relief. 'Thanks! But pretty soon it'll depend on his Gran. I'm returning to Africa shortly. There's so much to do there.'

'I'm sure there is,' she said a little wistfully. 'Only you must miss the kiddies a lot?'

'I do. But I know they're in good hands. Mum more or less took them over after we lost Glynis, they moved in here with her and I sold our house in Wales. It's a nice place for them, and they go to a good school. I'm very lucky Mum is prepared to do so much.'

I opened my mouth and shut it again, not sure what I had meant to say.

When Joe was rounded up to leave, and Grace was giving him a 'Cat Handbook' to read at home, I went with Darryl to the front door. Tonight there was quite a hint of spring in the air. The garden looked less like a wasteland, with daffodils rearing hopeful heads.

I asked, 'How is your brother doing?'

'Fine, so far as I know. I don't live there when I'm back home. It's Dominic's house, of course. He bought it and gave Mum free use of it, just before Glynis and her mother died together in a car smash . . . Mum said immediately, 'Those children must come here to me!' We just had to go on living . . . and the way it worked out, I was able to give even more time to the Help To Africa Project . . . '

Which, indeed, sorely needed his skilled and caring presence. And so would his two little children: Rhiannon then too small to understand, Joe who would have understood, and desperately, hopelessly grieved for his young mother . . .

'I've a small flat near my sister Ellen,' Darryl was going on. 'Mostly it's rented out. If I need a roof when it's tenanted, there's a handy b & b in Croydon where I stay.'

Again I opened my mouth, and again nothing came out. This all sounded very well considered and convenient. A plan that would run like clockwork — only clockwork was a chilly and inhuman mechanism?

It put me in mind of Dominic's dislike of robotic, mindless computers. I mused aloud, 'I wonder if he's finished off his play yet?'

'He hasn't. Mum says it's driving them all crazy. Making his temper even worse than usual.'

'Oh dear! You know, I've never seen one of his plays?'

'You haven't? Did you know there's

one on in Croydon at present?'

That would account for Mrs. Tremaine's valiant efforts to prevent 'the press' besieging Bramble Hill. The next moment, that thought vanished.

'If you're free tomorrow evening, why don't I grab a couple of tickets for us?'

It was an offer beyond refusing, even despite its inevitable complications.

After the visitors left, Grace was as thrilled as I expected when I told her about it. But she too saw hurdles ahead.

'Wonderful! Only — Beth, forgive me, but — did you ever sort things out with Toby?'

'I didn't. But there's no law against spending an evening with a friend. You could come too, I can phone Darryl — '

'My dear, you don't really want me tagging along. And I'm quite sure he doesn't!'

True, of course. I would have to be blindly stupid not to realise by now that Dr. D. Tremaine wasn't just seeking to boost the audience for his brother's work.

'It's so sad he lost his wife,' Grace was murmuring on. 'And Joe and the little girl, they do so need a mother. If you ask me, that's what poor Joe is crying out for.'

I hadn't asked her. But again, her every word had to be true.

Less than an hour later, Darryl rang to say he had booked the seats and would collect me tomorrow at seven-thirty.

It didn't leave much time to get worked up about my unexpected date. We were busy on Saturday: Mona sent an elderly lady to view our 'rescued' block — and Mrs. Williams formed an instant bond with the battered-looking Alfie, stroking him and talking to him, and then arranging a spotless blanket in an old-fashioned cat-basket that had probably known many beloved creatures over the years. It brought a lump to my throat. I was rather prone to that just now.

Alfie's departure left Granny in the sole company of a row of pretty young things. I told her, 'Don't despair, your turn will come, my girl.'

'Girl' was stretching it a bit. But she raised her scraggy neck to be tickled. Her usual scowl, which would be the envy of any panto villain, was less fearsome than usual.

I was ready well before seven-thirty. Not tonight the sober 'business' suit, but a plum-coloured skirt with a nice bit of swirl to it, and a pretty matching top. Grace nodded approval. She came out to wave us off in Darryl's car, beaming even more.

As we drove towards the sprawl of the big, busy town he apologised, 'Lucky I could get the seats, but they're not the best. I hope you're prepared for a three hankie job?'

'Oh, is it really sad?'

'It's brilliantly written. But it's sad. The last time I saw it, someone behind me let out a huge sob at the end.'

'Thanks for warning me! Have you

seen it many times?'

'A few. I like — ' He hesitated over the words. 'I like to hear the applause. I just wish I could bottle it and send it to Nicci.'

I asked awkwardly, 'Does he know — did you tell him we're going tonight?'

'I didn't tell anyone.'

It seemed strange. As strange as sitting here beside this man who was the living image of Dominic — and yet so different. These kind grey eyes smiled, gently, warmly. Even more they smiled, in the bustling foyer of the theatre complex, as he dived into the small shop for a fancy pack of chocolates.

I wasn't usually so tongue-tied. I mumbled, 'Dr. Tremaine, you do know how to show a girl a nice time! . . . ' Then I wished I hadn't said it, remembering the girl called Glynis, who should have been beside him now.

In our seats I looked eagerly at the programme for *'The Second Bed From*

The Window'. Included were brief notes about the author, with a photograph of Dominic frowning darkly at the camera — or maybe at all the world.

Darryl commented, 'Not one of his best days, I imagine.' I didn't know how to answer that either.

But when the performance started, I forgot all else. The scene was a deliberately claustrophobic six-bedded hospital ward, with sombre green curtains between the patients, with bedside lockers and flowers, family photos, bottles of squash — and a window affording just a tantalising glimpse of a sunny blue sky. During the course of the drama nurses and patients and visitors came and went. Just one of the patients stayed put, suffering a succession of major set-backs.

He had his visitors too: one especially, a beautiful girl who held his hand and talked about their future when eventually he was well. There were days when they laughed together, others when he pulled a blanket over his head and wouldn't look at her. There were days when he clung to her and covered those consoling hands with kisses. There came a day when the beautiful girl didn't come at all . . .

All of it was wonderfully, agonisingly observed — the cameos of nurses and doctors and cleaners, the endless round of meal-trolleys and medications, the passing dramas of other patients, humour and pathos, discarded library books, timeless tedium. At the final curtain he was at last able to walk — and limped forth alone into an empty world.

I had already got through a wad of tissues. The last scene needed a whole new box.

Outside the theatre it was shattering to find a bustle of lighted, busy streets, restaurants and clubs and bars. Darryl's gentle hand on my arm guided me to a pizza parlour, and we sat there with frothy coffee and Margheritas. He urged, 'Drink up, you need to after all the fluid you've lost!'

'Sorry! It was so real. And — it was Dominic's own story?'

'Some was fiction. That idiot in the end bed — and the adenoidal Auntie Glad always loaded up with shopping 'for your Uncle Bob's dinner' . . . '

'Oh yes, all those! But it really was his story?'

He didn't deny it. For a passing moment his face was deeply sad.

We talked about the children, and my work at the hospital, and his work in Africa. We sat there a long time, as though neither of us wanted the evening to end. But eventually we walked back to the car. The bright lights were left behind.

At the Cattery, he came with me up to the house. As I found my key he said quietly, 'Thank you for a lovely evening. I hope you enjoyed it despite the tears.'

'I really did. Darryl, can I ask you — the girl in the play who suddenly stopped visiting — was she fiction or fact?'

'Fact, I'm afraid. Based on Nadine Raymond, a young actress who starred in Nic's first play. I believe he loved her a lot. But Nadine had an exciting offer from the States — she's made several films, you may have seen her?'

'I don't see many films.' I added, without meaning to, 'Poor, poor Dominic.'

'Yes. But — I don't know how to put this without sounding brutal — maybe all his health problems have given him a highly successful career and a comfortable fortune? Without being so much shut in, he might never have started writing? . . . '

'And now he's laughing all the way to the bank. Only that's not true, is it?'

'Perhaps not. But — why are we talking so much about Dominic . . . '

He bent his head and kissed me. The kiss, like the man, was warm and gentle. He said softly, 'I hope I'll see you again very soon. Good night, Beth.'

My hand turning the door key was shaking quite a lot.

'That's super news!' I told Michelle. 'Really wonderful!'

'Isn't it just? And for you too, because I'll be home very soon — and you'll be a free woman. No more cats! Paris in the spring!'

Her phone call on Monday announced that not only was Trevor progressing well now, but his father was getting him transferred to a London hospital. She would be able to combine the cats with her bedside visits. It meant that my stint at the Cattery was almost over. In a few days there would be no barrier to booking my ticket to Paris and Toby.

However, for the moment, I was still here, still tussling with Obese Ginger for ownership of my room, still plodding around the cabins in my pink boots. But it was only the day after Michelle's call that the daily routine underwent an upheaval. When Grace answered the doorbell just after lunch, I heard her stammering in confusion.

'Oh! — er — yes, she's here! . . . er, will you come inside, Mr. — er — ?'

I found Dominic eyeing our mountains of *Tibbymeat* in the hallway with mingled amazement and distaste, as Skinny Tabby and Snowflake shied away from his walking stick. He looked weary, those imprinted lines in his high forehead at their deepest. The drizzling rain had turned his hair, incongruously, into a young child's curls.

'Er — er — will you sit down? — can I offer you some tea? — ' the flustered Grace was asking.

I amended, 'Make it coffee, no milk, no sugar, strong enough to descale a boiler! — yes, Dominic?'

That transforming smile, bringing sudden youthfulness to his face, glimmered through. The teasing voice said, 'I see you know my wicked ways. Thanks, but I won't stay. I just wanted to beg a favour.'

'What sort of favour?' I asked guardedly.

'I'm trying to deliver these leaflets for the 'Save Our Theatre' meeting. I don't honestly think I can finish the damn things. So — '

'You're tramping around people's doorsteps, in this rain? Why didn't you ask me before? Of course I'll do them,' I agreed briskly, 'but first I'll run you home, no arguments! Just wait while I get my coat.'

I dived up to my room. As I returned I heard him lamenting to Grace, 'Why do these bossy nurses always have to know best?' She laughed, still bereft of fluent speech.

Bramble Hill was barely five minutes away and five minutes back. He didn't invite me in, only passing over the leaflets and instructions where to distribute them. But I did insist, 'I'll collect you for the meeting, seven o'clock sharp.' He said with exaggerated meekness, 'If you say so, ma'am.'

Grace was still in a state of shock, most of all abject horror that she couldn't tidy her rather surprising house for the eminent visitor. (I reflected, didn't she think it mattered with Darryl?) All the evening she was muttering, 'My dear, whatever must he have thought! . . . I can't wait to tell Mrs. Trimble up the road . . . Do you think he noticed all that cat hair on the rug? . . . '

'We're a busy, working establishment,' I tried to reassure her. 'If he can't make allowances, that's his problem.'

All the leaflets were poked through the letterboxes that same day.

The meeting was scheduled for Thursday: a particularly hectic day because Montmorency, due to go home tomorrow, seemed poorly and I hurried him to the local vet. Mrs. Croft's Smokey was pining for his owner. Itzy and Bitzy had chewed up their bed and made themselves disgustingly sick.

I was late collecting Dominic, which of course he pointed out with irritating satisfaction. Well, he didn't have problems like those.

Having looked up the route to the hall, I zoomed along some back turnings, finally parking dubiously askew with moments to spare. There were a fair number of people occupying the rows of chairs. Dominic was pounced on by an effusive lady in flowing black and numerous amber beads, who spirited him away to the back regions. I found a place at the side of the front row.

If I had anticipated today's event turning out something like my dash to London for the sedate St. Mordaunt's College debate, a shock was in store. The audience was divided, some quite belligerently in favour of replacing the local old theatre building with 'apartments', some wanting a club/cinema/restaurant complex, some insisting the theatre must be saved. The harassed lady acting as 'Chair' was flustered and ineffective. The first guest speakers — a bumbling theatre historian and a dry-as-dust architect with facts and figures — received scant attention.

When the unhappy Chair announced Dominic Tremaine, I expected we would have a respectful hush. We didn't.

Tonight he didn't look bored and resigned. As though the occasion had actually fired him up, he gave a passionate defence of the theatre — 'The *live* stage must be encouraged everywhere — we have too much canned entertainment, we look at too many screens!' — and so on. But at the height of this diatribe he was near to being shouted down by a vehement heckler: 'You would say that, you make easy money from it! — some of us have to work for a living, mate! . . . '

How it was I jumped up to intervene, I wasn't sure. Whether it was the pallor of Dominic's face, or his grip on the supporting table, or the dangerous flash of his eyes, something bounced me urgently from my seat.

'Excuse me! — can we get our facts straight first of all? Did I hear you say 'easy money'? — do you know what you're talking about? — '

The defence of Dominic as a man devoted to a demanding calling, and my wonderful experience recently at one of his *live* theatres, poured out of its own volition. In fact, it achieved more quiet in the hall than there had been so far. When I ran out of words there was applause, while the lady in charge thanked me for a 'valuable contribution'. A few questions and answers followed, a 'next meeting' date was fixed, and that seemed to be that.

Two or three people came up to me to shake hands. In quite a state of euphoria I sought out Dominic, who also had a circle of well-wishers. It was a shock when he snapped at me coldly, 'So you think I can't fight my own battles, do you?'

'Oh! No! I — I was just trying to help!'

'Did I ask you for help?'

'Oh! No! But — ' I felt my colour rising, especially at the curious glances of people within earshot. But a closer look at his strained face seemed to explain matters, and I rummaged out the car keys. 'Come on, you're exhausted — let's get you home! — '

That added a gallon of fuel to a nicely smouldering fire. He flared back, 'No thanks, I'll get a taxi. I'm not one of your pussycats and I don't need your kennelside manner!'

Foolishly I mumbled, 'Cats don't have kennels.' He had already turned away.

Far less I was angry than quite devastatingly hurt. Surely I didn't deserve this! Not when I was just so anxious for him, when — the truth came to me now at this unlikely moment — when I was falling more and more in love with this unpredictable, infuriating, too mesmerising man? . . .

Walking blindly away down the emptying hall, I heard my name called softly from a corner at the back.

'Bethany! Please wait!' Darryl joined me, his gentle hand held my arm. 'I saw what happened. Whatever he said, don't take it personally, it's just Nicci.'

I nodded, struggling against tears as that guiding hand steered me out to the dark pavement and a chill night breeze. He said, 'I think we need some coffee. Or something stronger?'

'Coffee would be nice. I — I didn't know you were coming tonight? — couldn't we all have gone together?'

'I don't think so. I just slipped in at the back. I try to support him whenever I can — as unobtrusively as I can. Let's cross the road, that café is still open.'

I let him lead me to the lights and gingham-spread tables of Petra's Patis-serie, where we sat by the steamy window. I clutched a brimming mug gratefully, but I couldn't eat. I asked, 'Please tell me something. You're twins, you're meant to be very close! So why — ?'

He finished the question: 'Why are we a million miles apart. There's a reason. When we were just kids — we were like peas in a pod, everyone said

— Nic had an accident. A very bad accident, that's why he spent so many years in and out of wheelchairs and hospital beds. It changed his whole life, all his ambitions just went up in smoke . . . there were only operations and treatments and pain and frustration . . .'

His voice was unsteady. I realised I had touched an acutely raw nerve.

'I've tried to help him, I still try whenever I can. But he hates the sight of me, because — you see, it happened to *him*, not to *me* . . .'

'Oh, Darryl,' I whispered. Instinctively my arm was around him, comforting and consoling. 'That's — very unreasonable of Dominic.'

'Dominic doesn't do 'reasonable'.' He smiled bleakly. 'Please, don't let it upset you.'

Upset me even more, he should have said. Tonight had been already bad enough.

Soon after, he walked me back to my car. On the way he told me he would be away for the weekend, for a 'Confer-ence on Africa'. I wondered now, very genuine though his involvement was, perhaps it offered too an escape from his own family problems? . . .

In parting, he kissed my cheek gently. He said, 'See you again soon.'

Driving back, I kept pondering the explanation of the dark void separating the twin brothers, blacker and more enduring than the gloom of these chill, late-evening streets. His obvious dis-tress had stopped me trying to delve deeper. But still I couldn't understand why Dominic had such apparent hatred for so kind, caring, understanding a man.

Surely, I had been told only a part of a very disturbing story?

* * *

'Your Dad's doing well,' my mother said on the phone in the morning. 'His check-up was fine, they were pleased with him.'

That was excellent news. Less easy to answer was her concern about my own plans.

'You'll be running out of holiday. Such a shame if you can't get to see Toby!'

I hadn't told her the whole truth of the Toby saga, not wanting her to fret until things were settled. Nor had I said much about the Tremaine family. Rather guiltily I bumbled on about Michelle hoping to return soon but still nothing was definite.

After that, the day was fairly humdrum, with chores for the cats and Grandpa Garland's indigestion. I was feeling flat and unhappy after last night, turning over in my mind the parting with Dominic. It even depressed me that Joe couldn't come this evening because of something at school. I was just pondering an early night with an out-of-date magazine and some reduced-sugar cocoa (how boring could anyone get?) when the house phone trilled.

It wouldn't be Michelle. She had

already spoken to us twice today.

'Good evening,' an unmistakable voice said.

'Oh. It's you!'

'It is. I wondered if you could find time to help me out tomorrow. And — I'm sorry if I seemed ungrateful for your support at the theatre meeting.'

'I don't know about 'ungrateful'. You were downright rude, Mr. Tremaine!'

From the start of our acquaintance I hadn't minced my words. Now I heard what sounded like an amused chuckle. From the start as well, he had seemed to appreciate blunt comments.

'I'm afraid you're right. I do apologise for my filthy temper and boorish behaviour. Am I forgiven?'

'Well. I suppose so. This time only! What's happening tomorrow?'

'It's my sister Ellen's birthday. She lives at Eastbourne, and Mum intended driving down with the children and a load of 'Happy Fortieth' presents. Unfortunately Mum has one of her bad heads tonight — '

'Migraine?' I suggested with professional briskness.

'Yes. She can't face all the noise and fuss there'll be, so I'm going instead. Would you come along to help with the kids? Ellen will give us a nice lunch. You'll have a breath of sea air.'

Of all possibilities, this was the most unexpected. I said rather blankly, 'I don't know. I'd have to ask Grace, of course . . . ' The idea came to me, did he just need a convenient chauffeur? — but I didn't quite ask him. 'I'd have to help her with the morning feeds and cleaning, I could possibly manage half-past ten?'

He agreed, that would be fine. He waited while I asked Grace's agreement there and then. Of course, she gave it at once. I deserved a nice day out after all my hard work.

Discussing it later, she seemed sorry it was Dominic I was accompanying and not his brother: 'Such a pity Darryl's away, you could all have gone together!' I let that innocent suggestion lie. I also let lie the thought that had Dominic Tremaine proposed a trip to the Arctic wastes, I would be hurrying out to shop for polar fleeces.

It was a rush in the morning, but at least the sun was shining and Grandpa's indigestion had calmed down — two pluses for the day already. Just before ten-thirty I drove to Bramble Hill, having given the car a hasty clear-out.

But it seemed I needn't have done that. I was amazed to find an unfamiliar vehicle had emerged from the double garage and was being loaded with parcels by Joe and Rhiannon. Dominic was supervising. He was wearing a casual leaf-green sweater, the same colour I often wore to emphasise the auburn glint in my hair. For him, it achieved the hue of golden-ripe corn.

As he turned to me in the sunshine, his face was so like Darryl's, yet so different. The soul looking out of those dark eyes was ever solitary, ever searching.

I exclaimed, 'Oh! — is that car yours?'

'Mine. Don't faint, you'll block the drive. And good morning!'

So much for the unworthy suspicion that he just needed a chauffeur. I was almost offering to use my car anyway, but wisely choked it back. I was learning, slowly.

'Good morning!' I answered instead, and smiled a bright 'hello' to the children.

At an upstairs window I glimpsed Mrs. Boyle's sour, pinched face observing us. I asked Dominic, 'How is your mother feeling today?'

'Better but fragile. She needs to sleep undisturbed for a few hours. Joe, is that the lot packed?'

The boy gave him a dour nod.

'We'll stop on the way for some flowers. I'll just go in to say we're leaving, you can all be getting settled. And no-one squash the china, please.'

'It's that parcel,' Rhiannon pointed out helpfully. 'It's my present for Auntie

Ellen, I chose it. A mug with blue daisies on it.'

'She'll like that. Perhaps I'd better hold it in my lap,' I decided.

Her long dark hair was fastened by a pink velvet band. She was too pale, but indeed a pretty child — and aware of it, trying to see her reflection in the car window. Joe, grimly brushed and tidy, was plainly viewing the day with fixed gloom.

There was a certain amount of minor squabbling on the back seat. I sat in front with the parcel, feeling as though this outing was all a dream: even more when Dominic joined us, handing his stick over the back with the warning, 'Mind it stays on the floor, no fencing matches.' Rhiannon giggled. Joe didn't deign to answer.

The car had been adapted to suit Dominic's needs, and I found he drove fast and well, though at first I had to stifle urges to warn, 'Red light!' or 'Watch that lunatic in the white car!' Far best left unsaid.

We had some quiet, classical CDs playing softly. There wasn't too much conversation. I learnt that Auntie Ellen's house was near the sea and very nice, that Uncle Barry was her husband, and their children were Glen and Emma. Emma was good fun, but Glen never said anything. They had two cats (only two?) and two rabbits. It was Rhiannon who supplied this information. Joe's contribution was an occasional grunt.

It didn't help that we were delayed by an accident ahead. After that, Rhiannon was insistent on a toilet stop. Dominic turned in at a large garden centre.

'Do you fancy a tea-break?' he suggested to me. 'And we can get some flowers here, to save stopping again.'

Trooping across the car-park, more than ever this was a dream. We looked exactly like a family — but we weren't anything like a family. Someone else's children, and me a virtual stranger, and Dominic ever his enigmatic self.

In the pleasant coffee-shop the

children consumed milk shakes and biscuits. When they finished and went over to a tank of colourful fish, at last Dominic and I were more or less alone, face to face across the table.

He said unexpectedly, 'Thanks for coming. It's not much fun for you.'

'It's a nice day out!' I waved a dissenting hand. 'I need one! But what's wrong with Joe today? Not another set-to with Old Beaky?'

'Not that I know of.'

'Well, something's upset him. Doesn't he like visiting his Aunt?'

'Yes, he does. You'll find she's a rather special person, very warm, very wise. People go to her with their troubles and she makes them feel better. But, you see — Joe thought he'd be going today with his Dad or his Gran, or both. Not with me.'

'Oh,' I muttered. It was a frank and very sad admission of the rifts and frictions in the family. He wasn't looking at me, frowning into his inevitable black coffee. From instinct or impulse I laid a comforting hand on his arm — and he didn't shake it off.

I asked softly, 'Couldn't your wonderful sister help with your troubles too?'

'Ellen can sort out the hideously difficult. Not the impossible.'

I couldn't understand, only that there was so much contrasting brilliance and darkness in his life. I ached to do more than just sit here beside him. I was even trembling, because of my nearness to him, because of a sudden longing just to hold him close to me.

Rhiannon was running back to us, and the moment was lost. But a new thought had dawned like a flash of light. This 'warm, wise Ellen' must surely know what was tearing her own family asunder! If I explained to her that I loved Dominic, surely she would tell me?

'Let's get moving!' Dominic said abruptly.

4

The front door was open before any of us got near the bell. A cheery voice called out, 'Greetings, people! — Come along in!'

Rhiannon fairly flew up the path to her Aunt's waiting arms. Joe, suddenly losing his sulky scowl, wasn't far behind. I followed at a more reasonable pace with Dominic, who couldn't hurry anyway.

Away from this popular South Coast resort's town centre, the laid-out Promenade with its seats and planted beds and gloriously nostalgic band-stand, the house was genuinely five minutes from the sea. Its neighbours were mostly guest-houses, and here too there was a window card: *Comfortable b & b or half-board. Regret Closed Until June.* It was a tall, white building with floral curtains and pale blue paintwork.

I hadn't expected anything like this; as little as I expected the Aunt Ellen who awaited us, with a curly halo of blonde hair, a wide bright smile, scarcely taller than myself but at the moment very obviously pregnant.

Rhiannon was asking, 'Hasn't your new baby come yet?'

'Not yet. Sorry, sweetie!'

'I thought we'd be able to play with it. Can't you jump up and down and hurry it up?'

Ellen looked at me with a comical grimace. 'Hello, you must be — '

'Bethany Brown. I was recruited to help in the car. I-Spy, holding break-ables . . . '

'Don't tell me! Poor you! But it's lovely to see you. And here's my baby brother with these gorgeous flowers — all for me, Nicci?' She enclosed Dominic in a bear-hug that endangered the beautiful blooms he had chosen, laughing at my amazement. 'Didn't you know, Darryl is his senior by a whole half hour?'

I said, 'Oh!' Plain speaking seemed to be the rule here.

Inside, the house was warm, not very tidy, awash with coloured balloons and *Forty Today!* banners. Emma and Glen appeared from the back regions: the girl pretty, blue-eyed and lively, her brother tall, thin, nervously bespectacled. With them came their father. Barry Manders was almost comically an adult edition of Glen, greeting us uneasily, hovering well in the background.

Where the two tabby cats and accompanying house-rabbits came from, I wasn't sure. Of course, they captured Joe's attention immediately.

To satisfy Rhiannon and Emma there had to be an instant opening of presents. After that, the girls rushed upstairs to Emma's room. Glen followed Joe and the animals through to a conservatory extension where there were cat beds and a hutch. Barry invited, 'Er . . . er . . . Nic, would you like to have a look at my new computer?'

Dominic's eyes met mine and then lifted ceilingwards. I knew his views on soul-lacking electronics.

Ellen had already told us we weren't 'eating in' because 'Mum flatly forbade me to cook for the mob, she's reserved a table at the Old Copper Kettle as part of my present.' It was a nice thought. I said, 'Such a shame Mrs. Tremaine couldn't come today.'

'Isn't it?' Ellen agreed. 'Nic says she's much better, but she needs peace and quiet. We don't do peace and quiet here, Bethany!'

She and I were left alone in the comfortably lived-in lounge with an astonishing litter of wrapping paper and cards, half-finished drinks and dumped-down coats. I offered, 'Can I clear it up? You don't want to come back from a celebration lunch to this!'

'Oh, leave it. It won't run away. Sit down and talk to me, a nice girlie chat while we can! Nicci told me on the phone he was inviting you today and he really hoped you'd come. I hoped so too, I was looking forward to meeting you. You know, we all do our best for him, but he's a lonely soul. I'm delighted he's found a — a friend . . . ?'

She hesitated over the discreet word, and then went on amazingly, 'He's told me so much about you! The nursing, and the job you're doing now to help a friend — and the ginger cat who commandeers your bedroom! — '

'Obese Ginger. Did he really say all that? I didn't think he took much notice!'

She smiled at me that warm, wide smile of hers.

'You'd be surprised. He's a moody so-and-so, but he often rings me to chat — and since he met up with you I've noticed a big difference. That's the truth.'

'It's made a big difference to me too. I've known him such a short time — just days! — and I can't quite explain — '

'Of course you can't! Even Barry's computers can't figure out things like that.'

Again, that understanding smile. It was a heaven-sent opportunity.

'But there's something that worries me very much. Ellen, can I ask you . . . they're not just brothers, they're twins, they should be so close! And I know something bad happened when they were younger, but Darryl couldn't talk to me about it . . . '

She made sense of the muddled words. She nodded, looking silently into my face. I went on more shakily still, 'Darryl has been so kind, and he took me to the play about the hospital. It was wonderful, I — I thought it *was* Dominic . . . '

'You really care for him, don't you? Yes, I think you need to know.'

I sat there hunched by the littered table. From upstairs came the laughter and scurrying footsteps of the two girls. An old clock ticked heavily behind an array of cards.

The story she told began when the Tremaine boys were just a few years older than Joe. They looked like two peas in a pod — but really that was a delusion. In temperament they were far apart: Darryl ever in the background, studious and gentle-natured, while Dominic was always dominant, effort-lessly successful in everything he did — and he did a lot, winning sports awards galore as well as academic honours.

'He won a medal, 'Student Achiever of the Year',' Ellen said. 'It hasn't been much use to him.'

Fresh from that triumph, the family were spending Christmas with relatives in Scotland, and the twins went sledging with their cousins on some steep slopes. Dominic, of course, zoomed ahead on the biggest, fastest toboggan — and made fun of his twin falling off in a sprawling heap.

It was then that Darryl gave way to an impulse which would have, literally, life or death consequences. He 'doctored' Dominic's sledge to make it uncontrollable. Too late, he saw Dominic setting off with Ellen as

111

passenger — in a dangerous area the boys had been forbidden to use. Typical Dominic, and typically too he would have completed the run in flamboyant style . . . but for his brother's fateful intervention.

Ellen said now, 'I remember Darryl screaming at him to stop. But he couldn't stop, or steer, or slow down. I was so petrified I just clung round his neck, I nearly strangled him! — but he managed to push me clear and I was only a bit bruised. But before he could get himself off too, the sledge veered off into these big old trees. There was a horrific crash, he took the full brunt of it. For days after he — he wasn't even expected to survive.'

I whispered, 'That's horrible!'

'I know. I have nightmares even now. But please, spare a thought for Darryl. He owned up right away, and we all realised it was meant to be just a boy's prank — to send the conquering hero sprawling in the snow, nothing more! Maybe he's suffered as much as Nicci ever since, having to live with it. And — Nicci has never forgiven him. Never, never.'

Her voice was shaking. Her blue eyes were misted.

'Never, never,' she repeated. 'And I believe, living with this poison eating away at him has blighted Nicci's life even more than all his physical suffering. And he did suffer. Shattered bones that wouldn't mend — the awful fall he had through trying to get on his feet too soon . . . oh, let's not go there, Bethany! I'll just say, from being a model of fitness and success, overnight he became a long term invalid — and you can imagine he was never a very patient patient! . . . '

She paused again to steady her voice.

'Thank heaven, very early on I pressed him to start writing to pass the time — he always had a gift with words. Of course, I never dreamed it would turn out so well. Just recently he had a very handsome offer for film rights, did you know that?'

'No!' I whispered.

'And do you know how much he does for struggling drama schools, threatened theatres — and especially encouraging drama therapy for disabled children? Not only financially, but he visits homes and hospitals, donates prizes. All sorts of things.'

I shook my head. 'He hasn't told me any of that.'

'He tries to keep it low key. I think it amuses him to hide behind his persona of an evil-tempered, selfish, embittered grouch! You'll find he's all of that — but a lot more as well. Much more.'

This was a whole new picture of the man perhaps I really knew so little. For another long, long moment we both sat in silence. I was utterly shocked, deeply moved, by all of that revealing story. My heart went out to both the brothers.

'Bethany, can I say one more thing?' Ellen said at last. 'You won't be offended? Be very careful. I'd hate for you to get hurt, and Nicci has been hurt more than enough. He's not an easy person, I'm sure you know that already. Please — just be very, very careful? . . . '

Her voice trailed off as from above the footsteps and voices were hurrying downstairs now. Barry's hand was pushing open the door, his hesitant voice rambling on, 'So you see . . . er . . . it does pay to go for more memory, Nic . . . '

'Barry, sweetheart,' his wife said fondly, 'can't you forget you're a dull old geek, just for today?' She called aloud, 'Who's ready for a big birthday lunch, you folks?'

'Me! — me! — ' came a chorus of voices.

Across the room, Dominic's eyes met mine in half-pained, half-amused resignation, an intimate little glance for me alone.

Smiling back at him, I was still hearing his sister's so earnest warning . . . and remembering that another man's ring should by rights be gracing my finger instead of skulking guiltily in its box . . .

The birthday lunch was bright and lively. Perhaps, I thought, because Ellen kept it so. But her festive table, with its centre of flowers and its fancy cloth, really had two vacant places. Mrs. Tremaine, of course, was unavoidably unwell. Darryl was absent on his absorbing work — or because he chose to avoid family friction. My presence must be a poor substitute for a complete, united circle.

I sat beside Dominic, and his murmured comments reduced me frequently to schoolgirl giggles. Towards the end he produced his gift to his sister, delayed until now. There was a particularly ghastly card featuring a huge glittering 'FORTY!' The little box held a beautiful sapphire pendant. She came round the table to hug him.

After the meal, as the sun was bright in a clear sky, we went down to the beach. Quite a few people were about, strolling along the seafront, sitting on the seats with summertime faces. It was hard to believe that just days ago I drove down from Leicester in the snow.

Though it wasn't far to the beach, Dominic lagged behind all the way. Ellen lagged with him, explaining to me wryly, 'The future Miss or Master Manders is rather a burden to lug about.' It fell to Barry and me to supervise the children. Ellen had brought a ball, and the two girls and two so differing boys were soon scurrying around on damp, clean sand.

Ellen and Dominic were sitting on a bench at street level, but eventually she came down the steps to us. She told me, 'Go and join him. I can manage here.'

'Are you sure?'

'Sure.' She gave me a friendly nudge. 'Go for it, girl!'

I warned Rhiannon about getting wet feet, and then left them to it. As I sat down beside Dominic he was gazing out to sea with screwed-up eyes, the light emphasising the lines in his face that sometimes scarcely showed at all.

I said softly, 'You were right about Ellen.'

'Good. I knew you'd agree.'

'Are you warm enough here? What are you thinking about?'

'Yes, I'm warm enough! And I was thinking that you're a wonderful person too, Nurse Brown.'

It was the first time he had said anything like that. And for the first time too he took my hand, and held it between both of his. The storm-grey eyes looking into mine were softened, almost appealing.

'I was watching you playing with the children. It was a pretty picture. You were skipping around on the sand as though you were a child too. And your hair was shining like copper in the sun . . . '

I didn't speak, aware of my own racing heartbeats, afraid that this dream would break. And already the so familiar frown was creeping back, his voice sharpened.

'And now you're here with me, away from all the life and fun. But you don't have to be a martyr. I didn't ask you to sit here!'

I whispered, 'You don't have to ask. Don't you know I like being with you? . . . And isn't this better than looking at Barry's new computer?'

'Well, that's true. Barry is a well-meaning soul — but he can bore for Britain.'

We shared one of our little private chuckles. We went on sitting there, and he went on holding my hand. The family were close by, but we could have been on another planet.

All too soon the children had to be herded off the beach. Back at Ellen's house there were hot drinks, a birthday cake to be cut. Again all too soon, it was time to start the journey back.

In parting, Ellen hugged me and whispered, 'Keep hanging on in there!' I knew exactly what she meant.

The return journey was tedious. It only needed being cooped up in his

Uncle's car for Joe's sulky face to reappear, and Rhiannon was overtired and petulant. We ran into repeated hold-ups. Finally, Dominic dropped me in Bramble Hill to collect my car, with a brief, 'Good night, thanks for coming.' Just that.

I was hardly indoors before Grace pounced on me, agog for details of the day. I filled in some of them, and said Ellen had invited me to visit any time, especially when her baby arrived next month.

'But you'll be back working in Leicester?' Grace said a little wistfully. Though I agreed, privately I wasn't sure. I was as mixed-up as that.

Sunday didn't help much, because with Michelle's imminent return I wanted everything in perfect order — which meant a spring-clean of the 'animal kitchen', a review of the paperwork, additional grooming for a rebellious Princess, not to mention urgent vacuuming in the house. You could, I reflected, stuff several mattresses with the cat hair distributed around the place. It was a wonder all the animals weren't bald.

Joe was amused at the idea. He came for the afternoon to help, and he worked hard. I picked him up after lunch and dropped him home later, each time seeing only Mrs. Tremaine in the doorway. As well as helping with the cats, Joe had spent a while with Grandpa looking at the precious stamps, very polite and patient. I made sure to mention that to his Grandmother. It seemed to me Joe was very much a case of giving a dog a bad name.

Quite early on Monday I was picturing him back at school — and hoping he hadn't clashed with Conor Reeves — when Grace came hurrying out of the house. Busy around the cabins, I didn't suspect the surprise today had in store.

'Beth, on the house phone! — it's Mrs. Tremaine, she says it's important! — '

'Mrs. Tremaine? Oh, is it about

Dominic? He's not ill?'

The thought sent me rushing indoors. But the voice from Bramble Hill sounded quite composed.

'Good morning, Bethany.' (So I had reached first-name status!) 'I'm sorry to disturb you. Could you possibly call here for a chat this morning? Or I could call on you, if that would be easier.'

'I can come to you!' I said hastily, imagining the lady's expressive eyebrows soaring wildly on arrival here. 'Is something wrong, Mrs. Tremaine?'

'Not exactly. I'll explain it to you when you get here.'

It was vastly intriguing! Grace and I spent the next hour racking our brains while we finished the chores.

Just before eleven I presented myself for this unlikely interview. Mrs. Tremaine received me in her somewhat condescending way, ushering me into the room where I attended Dominic on the day we met. At present there was no sign of him.

She answered my dutiful enquiries

about her health: yes, she was much better, the migraines were a nuisance that came and went. She wasted no more time on that.

'I've a problem here, Miss — er — Bethany. I wondered if you might be able to help.'

I said guardedly, 'If I can.'

'You see, my sister Eva in Edinburgh is celebrating her golden wedding later this week . . . er — Eva is several years older than I am! . . . ' She was keen to point that out. 'I promised to stay with her for a few days. The friend who usually helps me out with the children here is otherwise engaged — but I anticipated their father would be around.'

'Isn't Darryl due back tomorrow?'

'He is, but now I find he's leaving again immediately — for the opening of a new fund-raising campaign. It's very unfortunate. I believe you still have some of your holiday left?'

'Yes,' I admitted more guardedly still. 'And I shan't be needed much longer at the Cattery. But I did intend going to Paris to see — an old friend.'

'Oh. I wondered if you could move in here for a few days, to look after the children and keep the house going. Ellen suggested I might ask you, she said as you're a nurse you'd be very suitable. Of course I'd pay for your time. You see, frankly I'm reluctant to leave Dominic alone to cope with Joe and Rhiannon.'

I was by now so astonished by this proposal that I could only mumble, 'You mean — you want me to *live* here?'

'For a few days. I'd cut my visit to Eva very short. But if you've already booked up — '

'Well, nothing is definitely booked.' My reunion with Toby was yet again drifting away over the horizon. And Ellen Manders was an angel incarnate!

For a while longer I remained there receiving instructions: I was shown a spare room at the top of the house which would be mine, and the children's rooms, and various details of their school and mealtime needs, their clothes, where things were kept in the big kitchen. Mrs. Boyle, I was told, would be in daily for cleaning and laundry duties. For any shopping I would please present receipts at the end of my stay. Mrs. Tremaine obviously was determined to keep things on a strictly business footing.

Just as I was leaving, Dominic's study door opened and he looked out enquiringly. He greeted me, 'Hello, were you looking for me?'

It dawned on me that he was completely in the dark about the planned arrangements. Well, it was his mother's job to explain, not mine! And I didn't linger while she did it, just smiling at him sweetly, telling her I would ring her later, and departing in some haste.

I hoped he wouldn't object to my presence in the house. But if I knew him at all, he would object strongly to any implication that he couldn't keep the household going unaided?

* * *

It was amazing how some very complicated logistics resolved themselves.

Michelle returned home, to squeeze the breath out of me and hand me a parcel containing a nice wrist-watch on a silver bracelet. 'From Trev and me,' she said. With it went a card, and Trevor had added a couple of shaky lines: *'Dear Beth, sincere thanks for all your help to Michelle and her Mum, hope to see you soon.'*

Which was very nice and very moving, and all of us were more or less laughing and crying at once. After that we went on a tour of the premises, and Michelle seemed quite overwhelmed. 'A lot of it due to Joe!' I insisted. She said he sounded like a little angel. (She hadn't, of course, seen the Joe Tremaine scowl.)

Darryl also returned, just briefly as Mrs. Tremaine had explained, but he found time to call in to see me. That meant another round of thanks for agreeing to help out at Bramble Hill. We sat in Grace's homely living room, watched by Snowflake and Skinny Tabby, while Michelle and her mother lingered in the kitchen a very long time making tea.

'Mum wanted so much to be with her sister because Uncle Rob had a stroke recently,' Darryl said in his quiet way. 'I'd have cancelled my trip, but she wouldn't hear of it. I know you get on well with the kids, Ellen told me all about Sunday.'

'It was a good day!' I added impulsively, 'You should have been there! But I do know now *why* you keep clear of the family, why you're always working so far away . . . '

This was desperately hard to say. I went on uncertainly, 'Yes, Ellen told me how — how you almost killed your brother — and it changed his whole world and caused him so much suffering . . . it was so long ago, but you're still trying to make amends, aren't you? Working around the clock, watching from a distance while your children grow up . . . '

His face had puckered as though at a physical blow. Still I went on, 'Oh, you're doing valuable work, we all know that! But — don't you think Joe and Rhiannon need you too? And — doesn't Dominic need his twin brother? . . . '

At that he raised a protesting hand.

'He needs me around like he needs a hole in the head. The kindest thing I can do is stay away from him.'

'Maybe it's true at present. But — hasn't it gone on long enough? You punishing yourself and your family — while he broods himself sick and gets more bitter by the day? Please, couldn't you try talking to him?'

'Do you think I haven't tried?'

'I'm sure you have. But don't ever give up. For the children, for your mother . . . ' Almost I added, 'And for me.' Instead I trailed off in confusion, 'Forgive me saying all this, tell me to stop preaching and mind my own business! Only — it does worry me.'

He leant towards me across the table.

'Beth, I wouldn't have you worry for all the world. I'll always keep trying to make peace, only it just doesn't work. I try to kid myself that if he'd been fit and well he wouldn't have taken up writing and found this gift he has — but that doesn't work either.'

I had no chance to answer. Michelle was at last bringing in the tray of tea.

Darryl stayed some while longer, talking about Joe's passion for animal welfare and then, as always, his own work in Africa. Michelle, who hadn't heard any of it before, was deeply interested. He promised to bring some photos to show her. When finally he rose to leave, we all went with him to the door.

'Don't stand for any trouble from the kids!' he said to me, his kind, wistful eyes meeting mine. 'I know I couldn't leave them in safer hands.'

As he turned away, Grace called after him, 'Come and see us any time, we'll look forward to it!'

Back in the warm, littered room, while Michelle piled up used crockery, she summed up his visit with a reflective, 'Hm! ... so that's your quietly charming and rather nice-looking Dr. Tremaine.'

'Not *my* Dr. Tremaine,' I objected.

'Hm! I've a funny feeling he could be. I was watching the way he looked at you with those very nice grey eyes.'

'That's just what I said to her the other day!' her mother chimed in.

'And I see now why you're not rushing into poor old Toby's fond embrace,' my plain-spoken friend insisted. 'But can I sound a note of caution? Shouldn't you be off with the old before you're on with the new?'

I evaded, 'If you don't mind, I'm not rushing into anyone's fond embrace!'

'Hm!'

'And will you stop hm-ing at me? I'd better go upstairs and pack a few things ready for tomorrow.'

I escaped to the little room that had

been mine during these past days, and wouldn't be much longer. But it was a while before I began any packing. I sat down on the bed beside Obese Ginger and for some while didn't move, with thoughts milling in my mind and a mist of tears in my eyes.

The inescapable sadness of Darryl, his eternal lonely regret, was in those tears. The obstinate bitterness of Dominic was in them too, the proud, difficult man I wanted to hold very close, to shake very hard until that monstrous barrier between the brothers at last crumbled and gave way.

And then, while Dominic was still safe in my arms — I wanted to ask him if he loved me just a little?

It was just a fleeting dream. Only a dream.

5

'You've got here, then.'

Hovering in her doorway, Mrs. Tremaine was sporting a very stylish coat and very high heels, along with a harassed frown. A taxi was waiting by the gate.

In fact, I wasn't late. I pointed out, 'We did say nine o'clock?'

'Yes! But nowadays it takes such a time to get on to a plane. Well, I must leave right away — I was hoping we could have another chat. Now listen, Dominic is out now dropping the children at school, but in future you'll do the school runs, won't you? Is that clear?'

'Quite clear,' I assented.

'Rhiannon could be starting a cold, I told her if she feels worse to tell Miss Fielding. So you may get a phone call about her.'

'I'll take care of it, Mrs. Tremaine.'

'And see that Joe does his homework. And can you make sure Dominic doesn't miss any meals and get overtired?'

The last instruction possibly would be the most difficult. I promised to do my best for all concerned.

In a few minutes the lady and her expensive-looking luggage were disappearing along Bramble Hill. I was left in the doorway with a bunch of keys and several admonitions about the house alarm, the fire alarm, and an expected message from the gardener.

Well, it was different! I had just got used to the care of umpteen cats, and now these new responsibilities were weighing my shoulders. I sensed already that the animals might turn out an easier option.

Nor was this thought helped by Mrs. Boyle reporting for duty, arriving in a small black car with noisy gears. She seemed annoyed at missing Mrs. Tremaine, but most of all annoyed at my presence here. A hopeful offer, 'Shall I make us a nice cup of tea, Mrs. Boyle?' was answered grimly, 'No, thank you, I have my break at eleven. Until then I've work to do!'

She stumped off to the kitchen to repair the ravages of this morning's breakfast and mop the floor. I took the chance to bring in my luggage and put it away in my room. Not an unpleasing little room, but it seemed lonely without a huge ginger cat hogging the bed.

I was disturbed by a commotion below. Hurrying down, I found an infuriated Dominic, just returned, and a defensive Mrs. Boyle.

'I'd just like to bring my car in,' he was telling her, 'if you'll give me enough room?'

'That's easier said than done, Mr. Tremaine — when the young lady's left hers where I usually park!'

'The young lady? Oh — this young lady.' He saw me on the stairs. 'I don't care how you two sort it out, I'd like to get my car off the street. Preferably today.'

Which was my greeting from the master of the house. I followed Mrs. Boyle to the kitchen, where she was muttering to herself, 'temper like a hornet' and 'never a civil tongue in his head.' She could be right at that.

'Sorry!' I apologised. 'I'll move up the road. There's lots of room.'

'Would you mind not treading on my wet floor?'

There could be more than one hornet in the house.

We did get the cars sorted, and Dominic drove his into the garage. Before vanishing to his study, at least he acknowledged my presence further.

'So you're here to take over my household, Matron?'

'I'm here just to help out. It's still your household!'

He gave a sceptical grunt as he shut the study door rather firmly.

There wasn't much time to while away before the next crisis. The telephone rang in the hall. I beat Mrs. Boyle to it by a whisker.

'Mrs. Sims from St. Stafford's,' it proved to be, reporting that Rhiannon was quite poorly. I agreed I would collect her at once, identifying myself as 'Miss Brown, standing in for her Grandmother.'

'Oh yes, we had a note from Mrs. Tremaine. Good, that would be great.'

I found my coat and my keys, and told Mrs. Boyle where I was going. She snorted rather like an asthmatic horse, lowering her voice confidentially.

'She's an artful little minx, that one. You'll see.'

I left her to tell Dominic where I was if needed, and escaped from the house with relief (already, with relief!) to drive to St. Stafford's. I had already been told about its location: a brick-built, many-windowed building behind green railings, with tarmac playgrounds and a nice sports field beside it. I was soon announcing myself as Rhiannon's temporary guardian.

'Oh yes, Miss Brown.' It was Mrs. Sims herself who received me, brisk and motherly. 'Rhiannon seems to have a bad headache — and she looks very pale . . . '

The child was always pale. The headache, I wondered, just might have been inspired by her Grandmother's recent migraine?

A suitably wan Rhiannon was produced, complete with coat and school-bag, and I escorted my drooping charge out to the car. She did brighten up considerably once we were on the move, even suggesting we stop at the Pizza Bar for lunch. She also mentioned that the sweet shop sold strawberry fizzers which always made her feel better.

Back indoors, I checked that her temperature was normal, and then settled her in a big chair with an all-crying, all-laughing, all-wetting baby doll while I sought out Mrs. Boyle upstairs.

'You know I leave at two today?' she

asked me. 'I go to my other lady in Barnworth Way. Did you want me to make the lunch? — I often do if Mrs. Tremaine's busy.'

'That would be really helpful. I expect you know what Dominic likes?'

That brought forth another of her horsy snorts.

I went back to Rhiannon, who said she was a bit bored, and her head felt a teeny bit better and watching some TV wouldn't make it worse. In a weak moment, I turned on a children's channel with the sound very low.

As a savoury aroma was wafting from the kitchen, it seemed appropriate to warn Dominic of the imminent meal. There was no response to a tap on his door. Doubtfully I opened it a little way.

The big cluttered room, with its library of books and files, its view of the garden, struck a little chill despite a glowing fire. Dominic was lying on the sofa, his fair head pillowed on a big blue cushion. In sleep, a frown still lingered on his forehead, of worry or pain or frustration, perhaps of all three.

I coughed, and then again more loudly. His eyes didn't open, but he sighed and stirred. I started picking up some scribbled papers that had slipped to the floor, or been thrown there.

'Dominic? Are you all right? I just came to say — '

'What are you doing?' He was wide awake now. 'Leave that alone, I'm trying to work here! — '

'You were sleeping. Will you join us for lunch, or have a tray in here?'

'I'm not hungry, thanks.'

'Yes, you are. It's an Old Mother Boyle Special, you can't miss a treat like that.'

For a moment more he frowned at me. But a glimmer of mirth broke through. He agreed, 'It would be criminal, wouldn't it? The gastronomic experience of the year.'

We laughed together, just as we had laughed on the sunny seashore. I added, 'Don't be late, or she'll stir in more toads' eyes and bats' wings.'

As I turned away I noticed something that made the room seem even chillier. The orchid on the window-ledge, that had been haloed by moonlight blooms, was dropping them one by one. The shrivelled ghosts of them lay forlornly around.

As though I had spoken, Dominic said quietly, 'Didn't I warn you, nothing in all the world keeps its beauty for long?'

I didn't know how to answer him. I left him alone with his discarded papers and his fading flowers.

★ ★ ★

Michelle said, 'Hi, can you talk?'

I could, because I was in my room when she rang. I agreed, 'Just a few minutes, I have to fetch Joe from school. How's Trev? — and the cats?'

'All thriving. Oh, and Mona sent someone to view the Oldest Inhabit-ant!'

'You don't mean Granny?'

'Yes, this nice, quiet, elderly lady wanted a nice, quiet, elderly cat. So what did that animal do? — hiss, scratch, lash that stringy relic she calls a tail, and poor Mrs. Barton wasn't impressed. Luckily she fell in love with Molly.'

'Good, Molly's a nice friendly little thing,' I said with oddly relieved fervour.

Michelle really wanted to know how I was making out at Bramble Hill, but there wasn't much time. I did get to ask if Joe could still help at the Cattery: 'He was afraid now you're home he'll be redundant, but maybe you can fit him in sometimes?'

'Certainly!' she agreed. 'Do you know, Grandpa keeps on asking, 'When's the young lad coming again?' '

'They made friends. Joe doesn't have a Grandpa of his own. — Oh, is that the time?' I discovered. 'I must go!'

We arranged that she would collect Joe tomorrow after school (a handy excuse to see the Tremaine residence) and I would bring him back later.

Meanwhile, there was another dash to St. Stafford's. I took Rhiannon with me, as there seemed nothing much wrong with her. Joe was already waiting in the playground: I wondered which of the various shapes and sizes of boys might be Conor, but thought it best not to ask.

Back at the house, Rhiannon flopped down on the sofa. Joe's face had brightened at the news from the Cattery, but it clouded again as he dumped down his school bag.

'I'm supposed to finish off that stupid history. Daniel Phelps borrowed my book and I forgot to get it back.'

'That's a nuisance,' I sympathised. 'Is it important?'

'Sort of. Danny wanted to see mine 'cos he hadn't even started his.'

I objected mildly, 'That's not very fair, is it?'

'Yes, it is! He was out visiting his ill Grandma. Now I'll be put in the

Unsatisfactory Work Book. Again.'

'Oh dear.' I had visions of another summons to Mr. Beaky Bilson.

Joe was going on, 'Danny lives right near here, by the Park gates — the house with the gnomes. Couldn't I go round and ask him for it?'

I hesitated, certainly not prepared to let him loose on this vague errand. 'Look, I'll drive round and ask, if you'll keep an eye on your sister — and explain to Uncle Dominic if he asks. Yes?'

He agreed with gruff thanks. 'You can't miss their house. Lots of silly gnomes.'

'Gnomes,' I repeated gravely. 'I'll find it!'

Back in the car, I knew where the Park gates were, having passed them when out with Darryl. The house also was easy to find, with its army of figures marching up to the door. The bell was answered by a harassed lady holding a wailing baby. With surprising warmth, Daniel's mother said he was really

143

worried about keeping that book — and dropped her voice to add, 'Joe's been so good to my Danny, the poor love does struggle a bit . . . '

I saw why when Daniel handed me the book. The boy wasn't just cripplingly shy, but small and thin, with — I noticed at once — a hearing aid. He whispered that he hoped Joe wasn't angry, and I assured him, 'Not a bit! Don't worry about it.'

The wails of the baby made conversation difficult, but Mrs. Phelps managed to add that when Joe recently came to tea he noticed their cat had been bitten, and the vet said it was getting infected and Joe saved it from getting worse.

I returned to the car in quite a glow. I had always known Joe of the sullen sulks and insolent tongue did himself no favours: it was nice to know someone else had found what lay beneath. By way of celebration I stopped by the shops for some nice cakes, and boringly some 'oven chips' lest Mrs. Tremaine's state-of-the-art freezer didn't deign to contain them.

The glow lasted all the way back, and then stopped short. The minute I entered the house I knew something was wrong. Dominic, halfway up the lower stairs step by difficult step, greeted me, 'Oh, there you are! I've been looking for you, calling you! — '

'I just popped out because . . . oh, never mind. What's wrong?'

'I don't know yet. Rhiannon was screaming blue murder up on the top floor. I thought you were here to look after those kids?'

'I am. I will!' I edged past him and ran up to the landing, and then up the top flight. The door of my own room stood open. Inside was an overturned chair, a fallen suitcase (I had parked it on top of the wardrobe) and more or less pandemonium. Rhiannon was lying on my bed with one arm cushioned on a pillow, while Joe tucked a blanket around her.

I exclaimed in horror, 'Good grief, what happened?'

'She's all right.' Joe looked round at me. 'She piled things on the chair to stand on and then fell off — and things fell on top of her. It's just her arm. I'm keeping her warm because of the shock, and I got her up without moving her arm any more . . . '

For an instant I just gaped at him. Only for an instant. Later would come questions about why Rhiannon was obviously meddling with my property.

'You've done really well, Joe.' I sat down gently on the bed beside the whimpering girl. 'Rhiannon, you'll be fine, pet. Just try to say where it hurts. Did you hit your head? — is your back hurting you? — '

'N-no,' she quavered.

I was smoothing her dark hair back and trying to assess the damage when Dominic arrived. I looked round at him to explain, 'A little accident.'

'Is it serious? How on earth — ?'

'Let's worry about 'how' later! I don't think it's serious — and Joe heard her

146

fall and he's been doctoring her very nicely — '

'Has he! He preferred playing at doctors to calling me straight away.'

Joe gave his irritating shrug. 'She needed helping quick, didn't she? We couldn't wait for you to get up all the stairs, could we?'

'That'll do!' I intervened sharply. 'Shut it, Joe!'

Rhiannon was shedding a new flood of tears. Family friction was the last thing she needed. In fact, I was really on Joe's side: the boy had shown admirable presence of mind — but could he ever do anything right in this house?

'I think an x-ray might be a good idea,' I went on. 'I'll see to it all, Dominic — I'll run her along to the A & E. Joe can come with us to help. So — '

'So it's in your capable hands, and I should just stay out of the way. Point taken!'

At another time I might have told

him baldly to be less touchy. But I could see his real anxiety as he looked at the miserable child on the bed. Also, I was sure, more than the anger in his face there was deep hurt.

If my hands were indeed capable, they needed to be just now. With Joe's help the sobbing patient was wrapped in her coat and assisted below. I kept reassuring her, 'It won't hurt you a bit, darling.' Below in the hall, Dominic watched silently as we left, and I whispered to him, 'Don't worry, I'll ring you as soon as we find out anything.'

I had opted for the big hospital in Croydon, as that was a familiar route, but I soon wished I hadn't. We met solid blocks of rush-hour traffic. Joe was looking after his sister on the back seat, and I wished Old Beaky could see him. Also, that I knew better what to say when he exploded suddenly, 'I hate him! I hate him!'

'Who do you hate?'

'Him! My Uncle! That's who!'

'Joe, I know he seems harsh to you, but — '

'It's not just that. He says horrible things about my Dad! You don't know, you haven't heard him! . . . '

I understood the answer to that after my afternoon with Ellen, the tragic drama of the Tremaine twins she had described: *'Dominic never forgave his brother, never, never!'* she told me so painfully. Perhaps, when Dominic looked at Joe, he saw again the boy Darryl whose moment of folly wrought such harm. Perhaps he needed no memories, it was enough to live with that poison eating into his soul.

I said shakily, 'Maybe you should ask your Dad about it. And meantime — don't say insulting things to Uncle Dominic like you just did. He's had lots of troubles. He can't stand being treated as an invalid.'

Joe gave a totally unconvinced snort. Thankfully a red light changed and we were moving again.

Swallowed into the vast complex of

149

the Hospital, we found the Emergency Department busy and bustling. I saw Joe watching everything with absorbed interest. Eventually, after plenty of waiting around, it was a huge relief to find Rhiannon had no fractures, that she should rest and see her own family doctor tomorrow.

With the children safely back in the car, I lingered outside it a moment to ring the Bramble Hill number.

'Dominic, we're just starting back. Rhiannon is fine. Nothing broken!'

He said, 'That's good.' And then, unexpectedly, 'Have you eaten at all?'

'Not a crumb. When I get back I'll fix something.'

'Well, I've made us all some sandwiches.'

'Brilliant!' I applauded. 'Good thinking! Oh, and can I say something to you without getting my head bitten off?'

'Who would bite off a head so wise and beautiful as yours?'

I ignored that smart riposte. 'Why not get a stair-lift installed?'

There was a pause before he said quietly, 'I've considered it.'

'Don't just consider, don't sit there resenting the need for it. Get it done! I'll see you soon. Keep smiling.'

I heard, I was sure I heard, a tiny chuckle.

Understanding Dominic Tremaine was a major task, but not quite mission impossible.

★ ★ ★

The sandwich supper was reasonably successful. Joe was hungry enough to wade in, even though the meal was made by his Uncle. Rhiannon had a few nibbles but she looked almost asleep.

'Tell you what,' Joe suggested to me through a mouthful, 'you could swap rooms with me, then you'll be next to her instead of up the top.'

'That's a very helpful idea. Thanks!'

He went off to transfer his belongings while I got Rhiannon to bed. I hadn't really taken note of her room until now:

151

the pretty pink curtains, the wardrobe stacked with attractive apparel, all the expensive dolls snoozing smugly around, the cuddly animals and games. In the midst of it all, the child looked very small, somehow lost and lonely.

She was obviously frightened I might ask how the accident happened, and she quavered a confession. Wondering if I had brought any gorgeous clothes or jewellery or make-up, and finding none visible, she climbed up to investigate my luggage.

I said gently, 'It's not nice to pry into people's things without asking. I'd have told you, I'm travelling light and travelling plain! But you won't do it again, so let's forget it and concentrate on getting you better. Just go to sleep, pet!'

She smiled at me from her pink pillow. Her eyelids were drooping, but it took a while before she really settled, and I sat beside her until she was properly asleep.

I told Joe that his sister would be

much better for a good sleep, and nipped upstairs with him to retrieve my overnight things. I promised, 'I won't mess up your room!'

It was vastly different from Rhiannon's, mainly remarkable for the wildlife posters decorating the walls. The faces of sundry gorillas, rhinos and seals seemed more friendly than the dolls next door.

Below I found Dominic had cleared away the meal. He said a brief goodnight. I thought he looked very tired: no doubt he did feel responsible for the children under his roof, and the episode had shaken him up.

I had just peeped in on Rhiannon when my mobile trilled again.

'Sorry to ring so late,' Darryl's voice said. 'I just wanted to check on Rhiannon.'

So warm and friendly that voice, so comforting. I exclaimed, 'Oh! How did you know about — ?'

'Joe rang me.'

The boy was a surprise a minute. I

said contritely, 'I was going to tell you in the morning, not worry you tonight when everything's under control.'

I explained the hospital's verdict, and gabbled on, 'I do feel awful about it! — I'd only slipped out for a minute. Dominic is really upset too.'

'These things happen. Especially in our family. But it's really not serious?'

'Truly! More a big scare than anything else.'

He seemed reassured, and we chatted a little more before exchanging goodnights. I was sorry to let him go.

It wasn't the fault of the watching gorillas and company that I slept badly. Twice I fancied Rhiannon was calling, and once she really did. At seven I hastily silenced my alarm clock. Soon after I plodded up the top stairs to wake Joe, who looked as bleary as I was.

I took it upon myself to pen a note to his teacher explaining that due to an accident last evening, any neglected work was not his fault. At eight-thirty I ran him along to the school, leaving a dressing-gowned Rhiannon meekly spooning in Chockypops under Dominic's resigned eyes.

It was a grey morning, the start of a day that got worse as it went along — you could say, a fitting follow-up to my first hours at Bramble Hill. There was a very awkward phone conversation with Mrs. Tremaine. There was the gardener ringing, to say he would trim the trees today or tomorrow. There was Mrs. Boyle, her nose twitching like a bloodhound's at finding Something Had Happened and Rhiannon was being taken to Dr. Matthews. I did the taking, of course, and collected the ensuing prescription. The patient had looked very limp in the Surgery, but brightened up enough to point out which shop sold banana lollies and Grandma always bought her one. Or two.

Before I knew it, it was time to collect Joe from the school. By the look of his face, he hadn't had a good day either. His sister, in the back of the car, made sure to announce, 'I looked at TV, and I had jelly at lunchtime. *And* a banana lolly.'

'But Joe's good time starts now,' I hastened to say. 'Joe, I want reports on all the cats!'

The gloom lifted a little from his face. When Michelle called, he was already changed and ready. However, I still invited her inside, to satisfy her curiosity. She stood in the wide hall gazing around, suitably impressed, especially by the framed playbills.

'All very nice! But where's The Great Man this evening?' she whispered.

'Probably working. On no account to be disturbed.'

'Shame.' She made a disappointed face. 'But I see my new assistant is all geared up. Hi there, Joe!'

Joe was looking doubtfully at my friend's tall, bright-faced presence. He muttered, 'Do you really want me helping?'

'Certainly! And my Mum is missing you — and Grandpa too, let alone the cats! Shall we go?'

I gave her a grateful smile.

After they left, there were a couple of fairly peaceful hours. I wondered, was the lull too good to last? It was.

I went to collect Joe, not using the car as it was a pleasant evening. As soon as I reached the Cattery I sensed something was amiss. The bell wasn't answered, and eventually I used the key I had been lent. As I went in and called out 'Only me!' I could hear a heated argument. There were raised voices, especially Joe's.

'I haven't done anything! . . . No, I won't, and you can't make me! . . . '

I exclaimed, 'Whatever's going on here?' In the back room everyone was assembled, a worried Michelle, an even more worried Grace, Grandpa slumped in an armchair — and facing them a fiercely defiant Joe.

'Oh, my dear,' Grace hailed me, 'can you help us? It — it's so upsetting . . . '

Joe himself gave me a belligerent explanation.

'They think I stole some stamp album pages! Well, I didn't! And I don't have to let them search my bag when I haven't done anything!'

He was clutching to his chest the blue sports bag which he usually brought, containing a change of shoes, a notepad and pen, and other odd-ments. Michelle turned to me with one of her expressive grimaces.

'Beth, the stamps were all animal pictures, and Joe took a fancy to them last time he came — and today he was alone a few minutes in Grandpa's room and now they're missing. So what are we to think? We just asked him reasonably, but he won't co-operate.'

I could believe that. An indignant Joe and reasonable co-operation didn't go together. I said quietly, 'Joe, let's just get this sorted. You turn out the bag, or let me do it. Is that a problem?'

'Yes!' He scowled at me obstinately. 'I haven't done anything! So I don't have to have my things searched!'

Michelle lifted exasperated eyes ceil-ingwards. 'Well, this is ridiculous! We can't leave it like this. Grandpa is very upset, he treasures every page of his albums!'

'I know. Michelle, I honestly don't believe Joe would . . . '

'Then what's the answer? The pages can't walk off by themselves. Maybe he thought they wouldn't be missed.'

How long the miserable scene might have lasted was hard to say. But it was ended suddenly by Grandpa asking in a quavering voice for some water because he was feeling quite faint. In fact, the frail old man looked as though he might well pass out on us.

Grace and Michelle flew to him. The missing stamps would have to wait.

I told Joe shortly, 'Get your coat on, let's go.' To Michelle I added, 'Leave it with me, I'll get to the bottom of it. And I'm really sorry.'

She said, 'So am I.'

They were experienced in dealing with Grandpa, so I didn't linger to offer my aid. It seemed the most helpful thing for Joe and me was to remove our luckless selves from their premises as soon as possible.

6

The walk back was a procession, with Joe stumping along behind me. I didn't speak, feeling it wise to let him cool down a bit.

But back at the house, I held out a hand for the disputed bag.

'Please? Or do you want me to take it from you?'

'You can try!' he challenged.

'Or shall I ring your father?'

'Ring him, I don't care!' He burst out passionately, 'It's just not fair! I always, always get the blame for everything!'

Indeed, that was largely true. The boy's reputation for trouble sailed before him like a rebel banner. Of course, his frequent displays of 'attitude' didn't help.

With every intention of a civilised discussion, I found it deteriorating into a shouting match. There was only so much disobedience and insolence you could accept from a ten-year-old. In the big sitting-room he glared at me across Mrs. Tremaine's elegant carpet, backing smartly away if I made a move towards him.

At the height of that undignified scene I found we were no longer alone. Dominic stood in the doorway leaning on his silver-topped stick, his face very stern. I wondered how much he had heard, but I wasn't in doubt for long.

He said sharply, 'Did you forget there's a child upstairs trying to sleep?'

'Sorry. Were we getting a bit loud?'

'Very loud. I gather something's missing at your friend's house?'

'Ye-es. Pages from the old man's stamp book, animal pictures that Joe liked. But that doesn't mean — '

'And he had the opportunity to take them?'

'Ye-es. But that doesn't prove — '

He didn't wait to discuss what was meant or proved. He beckoned to the boy.

'I'll take the bag. Bring it over here.'

'You're not my Dad, I don't have to do what you say!' Joe flared at him.

'No, I'm not your Dad. If I were, I hope you'd have been brought up to behave rather better. Will you do as you're told, before I lose patience?'

'Joe, please — ' I started to intervene. But Joe was already responding in his own way. He flung the bag across the room, to land at his Uncle's feet.

Dominic didn't explode, as I expected. He said very quietly, 'Pick it up.' For a moment Joe faced him in outright defiance. Then, just a little shamefacedly, he obeyed.

'Now open it up. Show me.'

I was aware of physically trembling with apprehension, imagining the colourful sheets revealed in all their guilty glory. But the bag held nothing it shouldn't have held. Dominic said, 'Very well, empty out your pockets.'

It seemed unlikely the pages could be concealed in that way — unless they had been folded or cut. There came to light some dubious tissues, part of a roll of Aniseed Chewies, and a set of 'Wildlife Recognition' cards picturing voles, frogs and so on. Joe muttered, 'Daniel's Mum gave them to me.'

I remembered Mrs. Phelps, kindly mother of the vulnerable Daniel, who I met yesterday. (Could it really be only yesterday?) I confirmed, 'I know her, I'm sure she did!'

Dominic didn't query that. He asked me, 'You walked back together just now? — so could he have dumped the stamps on the way? Hidden them in someone's hedge to be picked up later?'

I exclaimed, 'Well, you do have an active imagination!' — which was stupid, considering his profession. 'It's just possible. I don't believe it for a moment!'

We had really reached a state of impasse. But Dominic knew how to end a scene when its climax had passed.

'Very well. Young man, you can go up to your room. Stay there, until you're ready to apologise for your behaviour here this evening — and you're ready to tell us the truth. Is that quite clear?'

It couldn't have been clearer. Joe departed with his blue sports bag and his Wildlife cards. Watching him, suddenly I just wanted to open my arms to him.

Dominic sat down with a grunt by the fireplace. I joined him anxiously.

'I think — we've got to be really careful how we deal with him.'

'We shouldn't be dealing with him! His sketchy upbringing isn't our problem.'

It was one of the few references to his brother I had heard him make. I said diplomatically, 'But we're responsible for him just now, aren't we? Yes, he has a temper — don't we all? — but he's really very mature and caring for his age. And I know he wouldn't do anything to endanger being on the Cattery staff! — Dominic, are you listening?'

He had closed his eyes, but they opened quickly, thunder-grey. Tempers and storm-clouds ran in this family.

'I'm listening. Were the stamps valuable? I'm happy to pay whatever the owner suggests. Double, for all the upset.'

'That's a nice thought. But it's not just the value — old Mr. Garland treasures his collection so much, he was delighted when Joe sat down to look at them and ask intelligent questions . . . '

I halted there at yet another inopportune jangle from my busy phone. As I rummaged it out I longed for the caller to be Michelle telling me there had been some kind of mistake. Then I discovered exactly how untimely that call was.

I burst out, 'Where on earth have you been all this time, Toby? I've sent messages — written notes — '

The familiar voice said, 'Forgive me, sweetheart, I feel like the world's biggest rat . . . ' Toby's own brand of contrition always was enough to melt towering icebergs. 'I meant to rush over to see you, I just haven't managed it! — '

'And I was planning to be in Paris this week, but — it all went wrong,' I explained inadequately.

'Well, can you talk now? Is this a good moment?'

It was about the worst moment possible. I was sitting only a yard from Dominic, and he had sharp ears. Toby had a carrying voice.

'We've got to talk,' I said rather desperately, 'but not now! I'll ring you! Very soon!'

Whatever he answered, I never knew. I just cut the call off, aware of Dominic's eyes intent on my face. There flashed into my mind a vision of the first time he invited me into his study and showed me his precious pile of written pages: 'It's a love story called *Pale Orchid*, even the wonderful orchid blooms that seem everlasting have their time to die . . . ' Out of the blue I had revealed to a stranger all my hurt and loneliness of a broken love, and he answered simply, 'Me too!' A sad little bond between us that had so magically endured and strengthened. At least, in my own heart it had . . .

I said miserably, 'Can I explain about Toby? We — we used to be . . . '

'Please.' He lifted a hand. 'It's not my business. You're here by agreement with my mother to look after the children — so I suggest you get on with it.'

He eased himself out of the chair and left the room.

For so long I had yearned for just a word from Toby! And now it had come, not just too late, but disastrously so. For several stunned moments I sat there in the empty room, until I pulled myself together and went upstairs to check on Rhiannon. Thankfully, she was fast asleep.

There had been no chance to swap rooms again with Joe, which meant I was still with his animal gallery and he was in my attic. I tapped on the door and was answered by a gruff, 'Go away!'

'It's only me. Shall I bring you some supper?'

167

'Don't want any.' He added, 'Don't suppose I'm allowed to eat, anyway.'

I pushed the door open. Sitting hunched on the edge of the bed, he rounded on me, 'You see what I mean about him, don't you? He hates my Dad and he hates me! I wish I didn't have to live here, I could just stay at Aunt Ellen's!'

'Joe, try to calm down and listen. I don't believe you took those stamps.'

'Of course I didn't! Old Mr. What's-it is nice, he told me about a dog he used to have — it was called Prince and it lost an eye, there's a photo of it in his room . . . Well, do you think I'd make him ill by nicking his things?'

'No, I don't. And I'll try to convince them at the Cattery. And your Uncle too — '

He snorted, 'Some hopes!'

'Let's swap our rooms back, shall we? You'll be more comfortable, and if Rhiannon calls you can come to tell me. And I'll fetch you some supper!'

He muttered, 'If you like. Thanks!'

I felt a shade happier about him when the arrangements were made. But with the younger Tremaine fixed up, there was still the senior to cope with. I found Dominic making himself a sinister looking coffee and a sandwich in the kitchen. (Sandwiches seemed to be his speciality?)

'Can I fix you something?' I offered.

'Not really part of your duty rota, is it?'

I heaved a deep sigh and then exploded, 'This is downright stupid!'

It was stupid: perhaps because our two worlds were a universe apart, or because all that had ever passed between us was to hold hands on a sunny beach, to share moments of laughter, to find now and then an uncanny togetherness in glance or word. If he was accusing me of two-timing him with another man, there was very little to two-time!

At present I wanted just to knock his proud, obstinate, vulnerable head against the wall until an iota of commonsense crept into it. As he cut his sandwich into four precise sections, almost I hoped it would choke him.

'Dominic.' I forced my voice to quietness. 'Just tell me something! Is it really fair to blame Joe for — being his father's son?'

I could see the words jarred a raw nerve. He didn't answer me, and I didn't repeat them. I went straight up to my room.

Another small part still remained of that nightmare day. It was yet another phone call, just as I was deciding to fall into bed. Another call, but again not a 'Eureka!' from Michelle. Darryl's soft voice said, 'Apologies for ringing so late, but I wanted to ask about Rhiannon — and how today has been for you?'

That warm, gentle, sympathising voice! — but it brought me panic. As though Rhiannon's accident weren't enough, how could I explain to Joe's father the unpleasant accusations against his son?

I couldn't lie, nor yet blurt out the whole stark truth. Today hadn't been good, I admitted. Rhiannon had stayed home from school. Joe had a 'disagreement' (could you call it that?) at the Cattery. It didn't sound too serious put like that, but maybe some of the panic was in my voice.

We didn't talk for long. His parting, 'Good night, Beth, try to sleep well,' sounded worried.

Well, I had done my best. All day I had done my best! — but where had it got me, or any of the Tremaine family?

* * *

Dropping Joe at school in the morning, I saw Daniel Phelps sidle up to him with a nervous smile of greeting. Perhaps it would lift Joe's spirits. He looked as though he hadn't slept well, which wasn't surprising.

Rhiannon was still at home, with her sore arm and wan face. If I were being taken for a ride, no matter. In a couple

171

more days her Grandmother would be home again. Meantime, the child had had a bad experience, and a little pampering in the peace of Bramble Hill would do no harm.

Or at least, there was supposed to be peace in the big house. Today, there wasn't much. That wasn't due to Dominic: I scarcely saw him, and when I did he was coldly civil — and a million miles away. But punctual to the minute Mrs. Boyle arrived, commented darkly on Rhiannon — 'Didn't I warn you, that one's an artful little minx!' — and then began some very noisy vacuuming.

In the midst of it, I answered the house phone and almost unbelievably heard a not unfamiliar voice: 'Miss Brown? — hello again, Mrs. Sims from St. Stafford's. I'm ringing about Joe Tremaine, he's quite unwell today.'

I exclaimed, 'Good grief!' The woman must think I was adding something noxious to the family's morning cornflakes. 'Joe's rather upset just now — a family problem . . .'

She thought it would be a good idea if I came along to collect him.

I told Dominic where I was going, and he didn't react. Mrs. Boyle was avidly curious — possibly with good reason, with the children falling like ninepins. Just as I was leaving, with Rhiannon as passenger, a small green van rolled up and a grey-haired, leather-faced man emerged. Mr. Cheeseman, the gardener, he announced, as arranged.

'Fine!' I said. 'Just carry on, there are people in the house.'

It was a familiar route now to St. Stafford's, and a familiar mission. Joe admitted to a severe headache — probably due to lack of sleep — but to my mind he seemed more utterly peeved than unwell. Rhiannon welcomed him to the car with an aggrieved, 'You're not ill, I'm ill, and all these cushions are mine!'

'That's quite enough, just be quiet!' I remonstrated.

She whimpered that if I was mean to her she would tell her Grandma. In fact, I was amassing a whole new respect for Mrs. Tremaine.

In the house, the raucous vacuuming was continuing at increased decibels. In the back garden, Mr. Cheeseman was operating a mechanical saw on some overgrown branches. I gave Joe something for the headache, but a hint that he make himself comfortable in the lounge was flatly refused.

'Can't, can I? I've got to stay upstairs, haven't I?'

Yesterday's arbitrary banishment indeed hadn't been rescinded. For now, I let him stump off to his room. Meanwhile it was lunchtime, and there was no lunch in the offing. Unless — bright idea! — I made sandwiches? . . .

While I was sorting out ingredients in the kitchen, the doorbell rang. I was ready to give any itinerant salesperson an earful. But it was a tall, fair-haired, grey-eyed man who stood there in the porch and smiled at me. The smile was warm, gentle, like a balm of comfort in time of trouble.

'Darryl! . . . it's you! . . . but — *how* did you get here? — '

'I'm really not a ghost,' he reassured me. 'Last night, I thought — well, you sounded like you had too many problems. I felt I should drop everything and come.'

I was within an inch of just falling into his arms and weeping on his shoulder.

'Oh, everything's gone so wrong! You must think I'm a hopeless waste of space!'

'Of course I don't. But maybe you do need a little help.'

He had come into the house, and it was at that moment that Dominic peered out enquiringly from his study. For what seemed an age the two brothers exchanged a long, silent gaze.

It was the first time I had seen the twins together. The likeness — and the difference — was very striking. My heart was racing as I waited for the coming storm. But at last Darryl said quietly, 'Hello, Nicci, how are you?'

'I'm well. But I don't remember inviting you here.'

'You didn't. I came to straighten out these problems with the children.'

Dominic said, 'Not before time!' as he turned away.

Darryl grimaced, though he dismissed the jibe wryly, 'Oh well, he always was a sarcastic so-and-so. Beth, I'm sorry you're having such a bad time.'

'I'm the one to be sorry! Rhiannon is still home sick — and now Joe's home too but I think he's more upset than ill, because of the rumpus at the Cattery and Dominic banishing him to his room . . . Oh, I don't know how to tell you about all that! — '

He stopped me in full flow. 'First of all, stop taking all the blame. It's just the way this family behaves.'

I whispered, 'It's nice of you to say so.' What happened next, I really couldn't account for. He put a comforting arm around me, and suddenly I clung to him. The sense of warmth and support and kindness brought tears brimming in my eyes. Even more, it brought sudden wild visions into my mind.

Beyond doubt, this man did care for me. This man for whom I had already affection and respect, for whom surely I could soon learn to feel love? . . . who needed so much a mother for his children and a new beginning to his shadowed life. He was a doctor and I a nurse, I could share his world in so many ways — give him real help in his work as well as a loving family home. It would be so easy, so very easy! Just a word of response to his touch and his smile, just a little encouragement for these gentle arms — and then no more storm-clouds and battles of wills, no more Dominic frowns and moods and hurts and tears . . .

I was just aware of nestling closer, to the enclosing arms holding me more tightly. But the moment was crudely ended by a very loud cough from the stairs. Mrs. Boyle repeated her vastly disapproving 'Er-hmm!' twice more for extra effect.

'Miss Brown . . . er-hmmm! . . . I'm leaving shortly, is there anything else you want done?'

I couldn't command my voice, and it was Darryl who told her, 'No, thanks, leave now if you want.' Evidently knowledge of his presence had by now reached Rhiannon, because suddenly she rushed from the lounge to land in a sobbing heap in the arms I had just hastily vacated.

'Daddy! — oh, Daddy, I got ever so hurt! — I went to the hospital — '

'I know,' he soothed her. 'Never mind, we'll soon have you all better.'

For the moment, none of us was better: Mrs. Boyle was coughing still more as she donned her coat — and this time not due to what she would call 'goings on' in the hall. Pungent waves of smoke were filtering all around us. Rhiannon's sobs turned to panic as she wailed, 'We'll be burnt up! — the house is all burning!'

'It's not yet,' Mrs. Boyle said tartly, 'but you want to keep an eye on him in the garden, Miss Brown. All those branches he's set alight, it's a danger to health and safety! I'll see you tomorrow, then.'

As she spluttered her way out, Dominic called to me sharply from his doorway, 'Did you give that clown out there permission to hold his own Guy Fawkes night?'

'No! Shall I go out and tell him — ?'

'I'll go! We've enough to cope with here without adding a pyromaniac!'

He limped his angry way through to the back of the house. Darryl gave me again that wry look of his.

'You couldn't make it up. We could earn ourselves a fortune as a TV sitcom.'

Perhaps when it was all over I might see a funny side. At present I was too deeply upset — about what had just happened between the two of us, about the tearful little girl, about the whole series of disasters encompassing the household since I arrived on its doorstep with my luggage and my good intentions.

I wasn't especially thinking about Joe.

At this moment, were any of us thinking about Joe? . . .

★ ★ ★

The garden episode ended with angry voices and Mr. Cheeseman gathering up his equipment and marching back to his van. The vehicle departed at speed along Bramble Hill. The over-sized bonfire was still burning.

I wondered whether to take out a bucket of water — or there must be a hose available to dowse the thing. But I was tied up with Rhiannon. Her father had melted away somewhere, probably with the same idea about the hose. I led the child to the kitchen, bathed her face, and then sat her at the table with a bowl of her beloved pink ice-cream.

The place was still smoke-laden, but

it was quiet. The lull seemed to me quite encouraging. By now I should have known better.

Just as I returned to making the sandwiches, the door was pushed open. I started brightly, 'Hi, Dominic, I'm just doing us some lunch — ' and then stopped. 'What's wrong?'

'Did you go into my room and meddle with my papers?'

'Me? Certainly not!'

'Then do you know who did?'

I shook my head, in growing alarm. 'But don't you keep the door locked? You — you don't mean the play? — '

'I forgot the door when I went out to that damn gardener. Yes, I do mean the play. It's gone from the desk. Just one loose page left on the floor by whoever removed it . . . ' He trailed off suddenly, and I followed his gaze through the kitchen window overlooking the expanse of the big garden.

Armed with a businesslike rake Darryl was standing by the remains of the fire, which seemed to have flared again exuberantly. There were clouds of charred fragments drifting about like snow on a rising breeze. Somehow they didn't look much like wood ash.

As my horrified eyes met Dominic's, he swore softly, not mildly. Then he was on his way out to the garden. If he had hurried to deal with Mr. Cheeseman, that was nothing to the speed he managed now.

Rhiannon said primly, with more than a touch of her Grandma, 'Uncle Nicci said a naughty word. Joe got sent to bed for saying that.'

'Never mind. Just stay here and finish your ice-cream, yes?'

I wasn't far behind Dominic. Nightmare was following nightmare, and this one looked like topping all the rest.

Running across the grass I choked in the smoky haze. Even more I choked at the nearer view of those scorched flakes of paper drifting around me. On some, signs of handwriting were still visible.

The two brothers stood face to face, the one holding a sturdy walking stick, the other a metal-pronged rake. For one ghastly instant I visualised physical combat and bodily harm. That didn't happen. The taller of the two was backing away defensively: I saw Darryl's face, his kind and gentle face, taut and pale with apprehension.

Dominic said with admirable restraint, 'You needn't tell me, I can see for myself. You could have destroyed anything else I possess in the world. This was irreplaceable.'

There were no denials, no protests, just that miserable white face and the downcast eyes. I couldn't hold back a fierce tide of condemnation.

'Well, I know you two have had your own civil war going on for years when you ought to know better! But this is just appalling, this is — cruel and cowardly and despicable! Darryl, I thought you were a reasonable human being! How could you even think of such a wicked, wicked thing?'

Again, no protest, no denial. It was Dominic who answered, still with that

183

amazing forced calm.

'Don't upset yourself. What's done is done. Darryl, I've just one thing to say to you. Get out of my house, now, today. Don't ever show your face here again. And — while you're about it, take your troublesome brood of kids with you.'

I almost wailed, 'No, they've done nothing! For pity's sake, you can't just throw them out of their home!'

Darryl muttered at last, 'Please leave it, Bethany.' Just that, no more.

'No, I can't leave it! I'm supposed to be caring for them, and I'm not letting their poor little lives be torn apart because of your quarrels. Before they go anywhere, you'll have to drag me out first, inch by inch!'

I started straight back to the house at quite a frantic run. Let the two warring brothers fight their battles how they chose, they were grown men — or supposed to be! But I would protect the children in any way I could. Maybe I should ring Ellen for help? — or even just bundle Joe and Rhiannon into my car here and now to drive them down to her hospitable family roof? . . .

At the door Rhiannon met me to announce importantly, 'Joe's hurt his hand. He was sort of crying. He said he wasn't, but he was.'

'Where is he?'

Upstairs, she said. I grabbed her hand, and we hurried up together. The bathroom door was ajar and there was a sound of running water: as I opened the door wider, Joe wheeled guiltily round from Mrs. Tremaine's handsome pale-mint washbasin. He was running cold water on his hand.

'What happened to you? Let me see,' I invited him, and then made a grab for the arm he was trying to conceal. The boy's hand was reddened and already hinting at tell-tale blisters. 'That's a nasty burn! But how did you — ? Oh!'

There was no need to finish the question. He answered it boldly.

'Yes, I did it. I burnt up all his stupid old papers — and I don't care!'

I was totally, utterly shocked. Perhaps even more now than out in the garden among the scattering ashes.

'Joe . . . I don't know what to say. Do you even begin to realise what you've done? — they weren't 'old papers', it was the play he's been working on for a very long time . . . And there's something else you should know. Listen, just now your Dad was taking all the blame for destroying it!'

He was still defiant, but that seemed to shake him. He muttered, 'He didn't do it, I did. I saw the fire through the window, and no-one was there except the cat from down the road and it could get hurt — so I went down, and that door was open for once — so I just grabbed the stuff off the desk, I thought it would pay him out for calling me a thief! . . . '

Like father, so like son. A double lightning-strike of mad folly that couldn't be recalled. Both times Dominic had been the victim, had inspired the dark impulse.

I asked more gently now, 'So do you want your father taking the blame? Joe, years ago he played a silly trick that went horribly wrong, it's made him very unhappy ever since. He's a very, very kind person, he doesn't want you to live like that too.'

The boy was beginning to look utterly miserable now. I repeated, 'Do you want him to take all the blame for you? Or shall we go down and tell them the truth? Or shall I do it by myself?'

'N-no. I'll own up. I'll do it.'

'Come on, then,' I urged softly. 'Let's get it over.'

Whatever his faults, he didn't lack courage. On our way down Rhiannon trailed behind us, not understanding what was happening except it had made Joe unhappy. She tried to hold on to him comfortingly.

In the big lounge at the back of the house, the lace-draped windows looked out on the garden that was still hazy with smoke. Darryl was giving a final prod to the embers, evidently safety-conscious even at this moment of crisis. As he turned back towards the house, I banged on the window and beckoned.

Of Dominic there was no sign and I called his name in the hall. The brothers arrived in the room at the same moment. Dominic was about to walk away again without a word, but very dramatically I planted my back against the door.

'No, you have to stay! Both of you must stay!'

He said angrily, 'I don't know what game you're playing here — '

'It's not a game. It's very important. Will you sit down?'

He shook his head impatiently, leaning on the back of the sofa. Darryl stood quiet and still by the window. I didn't prolong the agony.

'Dominic, Joe has something to tell you.'

The boy looked frightened now facing his Uncle, but still there was lingering defiance. 'I put those papers in the fire! I did it, and I still don't care! You think I'm a thief, and I'm not, but it wasn't just that — it's because you're always so horribly *mean* to my Dad! And it's not fair, what did he ever do to *you*? . . . '

It was the one question above all others, asked all unknowingly, that spanned so many years of pain and bitterness. For one moment I saw brother look at brother across the room, or across time.

When Dominic spoke at last, it wasn't to Joe but to Joe's father.

'Just now you led me to believe the burn-up was your doing. Why?'

Another question that hung in the air unanswered. Darryl had put an arm round Joe, but his face for once was as obstinate as his brother's. The deadlock had to be broken somehow. I said shakily in the heavy quiet, 'If it helps, I — I think I can explain why. Ellen told me the ghastly thing that happened years ago, it was a young boy's stupid prank — like Joe's now only worse, because it nearly killed both of you! Yes, both of you! Dominic, do you really believe Darryl's life wasn't shattered too, living with such terrible remorse day after day, year after year? — '

No-one spoke. I had to go on, though my voice was breaking.

'We know he's doing valuable work in Africa — but why do you think he banished himself half across the globe, even though his family need him here? . . . And yes, he did try to take the blame for Joe today — because he doesn't want Joe living with regret and misery and disgrace the same way he's had to do! Can't you understand that, Dominic? Can't you stop believing you were the *only* one to be maimed for life? . . . '

The tension in the room was like some huge electric storm about to break. Rhiannon had shrunk back into a corner. But Joe, his emotions already in tumult, was shedding tears of mingled fear and still lingering defiance.

'Anyway — ' He sobbed out the words. 'There's — there's other copies of all that writing, aren't there? So — so — '

For the first time Dominic spoke to him, quite gently. 'There's no other copy. Two years of work are floating round in smoke.'

Joe's face crumpled still more. But in fact, Dominic seemed far less interested in him than in Darryl. He asked his brother abruptly, 'You were really going to let me throw you all out of the house?'

Darryl gave a bleak little smile.

'You couldn't have thought much worse of me. And — Joe has all his life to live.'

Another of those electric silences was beginning. Again, I had to end it.

'Darryl, can you forgive me for thinking you were responsible? — I should have known you much better . . . ' I took a deep, deep breath. 'Please listen, both of you. Tell me to mind my own business, but — don't you think this is a good moment to put a broken family back together? For the children's sake, it's their family too? . . . '

Across the room, the two pairs of grey eyes met again. It was Darryl who made the first move, coming quietly over to extend a visibly shaky hand.

'Nicci, I can't even begin to say how sorry I am . . . for so many things . . . '

For an eternal moment Dominic hesitated. As I watched I was desperately longing, earnestly praying, fearing with a physical sickness of dread a cold rebuff, a cruel rejection. And indeed, he didn't accept that proffered hand.

But instead, he took a halting step nearer to his brother, and another, to hold Darryl silently in his arms.

The twins shared their mutual embrace of reconciliation, just briefly, tentatively. For the moment, that was all. It was enough.

The heavens had fallen from their starry heights. The earth had stopped whirling on its axis.

7

Anything that followed had to be an anticlimax.

Dominic's stick had dropped to the floor, and it was Joe who nervously retrieved it. In doing so, he jarred his hurt hand and yelped, calling everyone's attention to the injury. How that injury happened, of course, was only too clear.

Darryl, obviously glad of a reason to escape, said at once, 'Let's go upstairs and attend to that, Joe.' He also rescued Rhiannon from her hiding place, to marshall both children from the room.

At the door, he paused to look round at me. I couldn't mistake the message in the little questioning smile.

Dominic wasn't far behind him, and in his case there was no backward glance, no smile. He looked more utterly shaken than Darryl. I heard his study door shut, the door just once left unlocked and unguarded.

Alone now in the empty room, the silence all around was like a living thing bearing down on me, stifling feeling and thought. I didn't feel, I couldn't think. I knew only that both the brothers, each in their own way, were waiting for me. The drama that had just unfolded wasn't over yet. For me, perhaps it was only beginning.

The sudden jangle of my benighted phone was crudely intrusive. I pulled the thing out to silence it, not really to answer it. But I did answer it.

It had to be Toby. No-one else could consistently ring at such impossible moments.

'Sorry if this isn't a good time again — there just isn't one to say what I've got to say! . . . Are you listening?'

I was listening. I mumbled, 'I've something to tell you too . . . '

'Please, me first! I can't sleep, I can't eat, I've got to get it said somehow!'

'You've found someone else, Toby. Haven't you?'

A whole flood of words poured out then: that he would always care for me, I was so special and we had shared such happy times, it was killing him to think of hurting me ... but there was Francine in the Paris office ...

Yes, I had been hurt. When I came down here first on a grey wintry day and Grace offered me a shoulder to cry on, I was hurting very much. Toby was right, we had shared happy times. Perhaps both of us had just read too much into them.

I tried to tell him, I had guessed, and I was surviving. He was begging me not to hate him as much as he deserved, promising he would still be there for me if I needed him. Typical Toby. I knew I would always care for him a little too, remembering our days in the sunshine when all the world was our playground.

But you couldn't play for ever. There was a time to grow up.

I told him truthfully, 'I couldn't hate you even if I wanted to. Don't worry about me, I've lots going on — I've met some new people too . . . '

If there was more he wanted to say, I cut it short. 'I have to go!' — and then, absurdly formal, 'And thank you very much for ringing.'

'No, thank *you* — for just being you. Bless you, Bethy.'

That was all. It was a day for rampaging emotions, and there were rivers of tears on my face. It took a few minutes to stop them flowing and mop them up, before I managed to leave my chair. On top of the past hour, this was almost too much.

Out in the hallway I stood quite still, just listening to the brooding quiet of the big house. In the kitchen my efforts at lunch must be a little weary and wilting by now. In the garden the bonfire still innocently smouldered. Upstairs, with the two children I had come to know so well, their father was waiting for me to join them, the man who had been so kind, who just once had kissed me.

It was to none of those that I moved

at last. I tapped on Dominic's door, and it opened under my hand.

Once, I had come here and found him prone on his shabby sofa fast asleep. Now, he sat hunched at his rifled desk. His bowed head was slumped on both his hands, his face hidden. I heard just one broken sob. When he looked round at me I saw my own tears weren't the only rivers flooding forth today.

He didn't speak, his drenched grey eyes dark with the pain he had hidden from everyone else but wasn't hiding from me. I moved nearer, and then nearer still. I whispered, 'Darling, couldn't you start the play over again?'

'You don't know what you're saying.' His voice broke as I had never heard it. 'Where can I get back all the time . . . all the energy . . . all what you'd call the inspiration? . . . Oh, the kid didn't understand what he was doing, I realise that! Our family go in for these mad moments, you'll have noticed. But — this one was madder than most . . . '

He lifted his head, making an obvious effort at composure.

'Apologies for the maudlin exhibition! If you've something to say, can you make it brief?'

Had he even noticed that tell-tale word of endearment I let slip just now? Or was he purposely ignoring it?

'Yes, I've something to say. And it's best you don't bottle up what you're feeling . . . ' I quite expected the grunt that received, what he would call 'Matron's know-it-all advice.' 'I've been remembering when you first showed me your writing, you said the orchid flowers wouldn't last for ever and we both said our own love stories had died on us too . . . I know now mine was a big mistake . . . '

He stirred impatiently, but I struggled on.

'The orchid will flower again. It will! And — '

'And guess what, love can bloom again too in a broken heart,' he finished for me mockingly.

'Yes, it can. I've proved it can. Because — I love you, very much. Only you, Dominic. Only you . . . ' The whispered confession sounded loud in the quiet. I floundered on, 'And — and I don't believe the play is dead either! Because — don't you see, now it can have the ending you couldn't find? — '

He actually waved that aside. 'Never mind the play. There are more important things. Bethany, what you did for us all today — you were magnificent, do you know that? We owe you our eternal gratitude.'

'Oh! I don't want any gratitude.'

'It's yours anyway. Mine, and I'm sure Darryl's too. But — tell me again, did you really mean what you just said?'

'That I love you?' I whispered. 'Yes, I do.'

'I see. That's nice. But shouldn't you consider it a bit more? I'm not exactly a model of health and beauty, you know. On the shop-soiled side — and people do say I've a temper like a nest of dyspeptic vipers.'

199

'They're absolutely right,' I agreed demurely.

There was dawning just a ghost of his rare, so transforming smile, a shaft of sunlight parting heavy clouds. 'Do you mind? — I get enough lip from young Joe . . . You know I love you too, don't you?'

I shook my head. I didn't know. I had only dreamed my dream.

'Yes. I believe it must have happened the day we first met. When you ransacked my garden and bulldozed me down the steps in a heap.'

'I did no such thing! — ' I started to protest. But the words weren't finished.

He said, 'That should have been enough to warn me. I'm glad it didn't warn me.'

Somehow then I was in his arms, and he in mine. Held very close to him, his kiss on my waiting lips was more joy than I had ever known.

★　★　★

Those first moments we had together didn't last long. Rhiannon came looking for me to ask if there was any more ice-cream, because her tummy was rattling.

We had eventually a rather amazing family lunch, all sitting down together to 'instant' soup followed by my forlorn sandwiches. Across the table the twin brothers exchanged only a couple of almost comically over-polite words. Rome wasn't built in a day. Far more it mattered that Dominic had invited Joe, 'Will you sit here next to me?'

Joe looked as uneasy as someone invited to sit on a bed of rampant nettles. This was another relationship needing time and patience.

When finally I retreated to the kitchen to clear up, Darryl came in to help. They were a difficult few minutes. It hurt me that I was hurting him: knowing him as I did, I sensed he would always be my dear friend in the future.

And part of that future he had already settled.

'I just had a very personal chat with Nicci, if you can believe that. He told me about the two of you. You're obviously good for him! . . . And I've decided I should be here more for the kids, so I'll arrange my work to spend more time at home. For the present, at least. There's plenty to do, fund-raising, recruiting, planning ahead . . . '

'Joe and Rhiannon will be very glad. And — Darryl, I'm so sorry.'

'Don't be sorry.' His smile was wistful, but he did smile. 'Just be happy. That's all I want for you, Beth.'

Was it just possible that in so willingly relinquishing me to his brother, standing aside without query or protest or persuasion, he had found at last some peace of mind in the sacrifice? I prayed that it might be so.

I was very near to dropping more of today's abundant tides of tears into the sandwich crusts when Rhiannon wandered in to hand me my mobile, left on a chair after I spoke to Toby. She said, 'It was making a funny noise. Daddy, I'm drawing a big picture — can you come and see?'

They went off hand in hand. Darryl didn't look back at me.

Tempted to kill that phone stone dead in a bucket of water, I was soon glad I didn't. There was a voice-mail from Michelle waiting. Very late, the 'Eureka!' moment had come.

'Grandpa is absolutely devastated about it — we all are! I don't know what we can say to poor dear Joe . . . '

It seemed the old man had removed the pages from the loose-leaf album actually intending to give them to Joe, to reward his work at the Cattery. He put them in a drawer in his room, and then totally forgot them. Only when Grace was putting away clean laundry this afternoon had they come to light.

'Please ring me,' Michelle finished, 'if any of you ever want to speak to us again!'

I didn't ring back right away. After a few minutes I went to find Joe, who was helping to fetch some things in from his father's car.

'I told you I never took them.' Joe received the news in a resigned, world-weary way: he looked utterly subdued, his eyes still red and puffy. 'I told everyone.'

'I'm so sorry about it. Look, if we call there to see Mr. Garland it might be really helpful? — if you could face doing that? He's terribly upset. And it really wasn't his fault — '

'I know. Danny's Gran is the same, she forgets things. She put her false teeth in the freezer. They weren't found for two days.'

Darryl said gravely, 'I hope they didn't eat up all the food.'

We needed a spark of humour somewhere.

The visit was best tackled right away. Darryl promised to report the news to his brother — which was a miracle in itself.

Though the distance was so short, I opened up my car for Joe. In only a few minutes we reached the Corner Cattery, where the painted board announced its services. It seemed a lifetime since I first arrived here, uneasy about what faced me, fretting about my delayed Paris plans.

'Bethany!' It was Grace who opened the door to us. 'Lovely to see you! And — Joe, dear, come here!' As she opened her motherly arms to him, it brought an ache to my throat. He almost disappeared in the warm embrace. 'Joe, we're so, so sorry about the awful mistake.'

''s all right,' he said gruffly.

'But it's not. Come on inside! — and you, Beth. Michelle is just giving Grandpa his medicine, we're in such a muddle here — well, you know how it is! . . . '

The familiar sacks and tins of cat food greeted me. Obese Ginger greeted me too, rubbing his excess bulk round my legs. Snowflake watched from the stairs. The impressive house at Bramble

Hill had its merits, but this was like coming home.

She took us straight through to Mr. Garland's room, where he was huddled on his bed in a dressing-gown, and Michelle was coaxing him to swallow down a tablet. As he peered at us over his glasses, his face puckered as though he was going to cry.

'Well, look who's come to see us!' Michelle said over-brightly.

It was actually Joe who took the initiative, marching straight over to the bed.

'Hi, Grandpa. Glad you found the stamps. Don't worry about it, all right?'

He wasn't answered in words, but the old man held out a trembling hand. Joe shook it very politely.

Grace was beaming as she cleared the bedside chair for Joe. 'Sit here a while, dear, you two have a nice chat. Then go and see the cats, if you want?'

There was no doubt Joe would want. I left him in these kindly hands and followed Michelle towards the kitchen.

She said, 'That was quite something, I'm very impressed. Your Joe is a real character!'

'He is. But — he's not exactly going to be my Joe.'

'No? So you still haven't fallen for that dishy Dr. Tremaine? Come on, I can see you're bursting to tell me something!'

'Bursting,' I confessed. 'I can't believe it myself. We had some sensational things happening today, and Dominic was very upset, and — I told him I love him!'

'Rash,' my friend muttered. 'So — ?'

We got no further. A ring at the doorbell made her put down the kettle half filled.

'That'll be old Mr. Hodgson delivering Tiggy. Will you be an angel and see if the second cabin along is ready? We're all at sixes and sevens here today!'

She wasn't the only one. I slipped out while she was answering the door.

It was a springlike afternoon, and the

rows of cat pens looked quite cheerful, their occupants snoozing or watching to see who was around. Tiggy's quarters seemed to be in order, so I stopped to greet some familiar faces: Smokey, Miss Biddle's beautiful Princess, Mrs. Joliffe's Bertie. There was a new tortoiseshell in the 'rehoming' group, fixing me with appealing golden eyes. I hailed it, 'Hello there, beautiful!'

'And hello to you, gorgeous,' a voice responded.

It wasn't the tortoiseshell cat. Nor would it be Tiggy or his elderly owner. I wheeled round to stare in disbelief at Dominic.

'What — what are you doing here?'

'I spotted your car driving off. I was afraid you'd had a change of heart and were doing a runner. You weren't, I hope?'

'Nothing of the sort! I just brought Joe to see Grandpa — did Darryl tell you the stamps were found? Joe was a star, the way he behaved with Mr. Garland.' I appealed with sudden earnestness, 'This seems like a day for big forgiving — so could you manage to forgive Joe? And tell him so? On the way here he said he's really sorry, he wants to talk to you.'

'Yes, I'll talk to him. I daresay I've been harsh with him. But — he didn't have to do what he did . . . ' He drew a deep, sighing breath. 'Well, no use looking back. I've been doing some thinking, making some plans. Shall I tell you? *Pale Orchid* will have a rebirth, it's a mammoth task but I'll try. Only, before I start — you do still have some holiday left?'

'Just a few days. Why?'

'I've some very hospitable friends I've known for years, Guido and Bianca live near Venice. Why don't I give them a call and then we can hop on a plane and visit them?'

'You mean — go to Italy? Just you and me?'

'Just us. Is that a problem?'

Dazedly I shook my head. He had more to say.

'Meantime, I intend telling Darryl he can move into Bramble Hill with Mum and the kids. It seems a good answer, they'll all be happy about it. And I'll work much better at my other address. It's called 'Rose Cottage' and it's chocolate-box beautiful. Wonderful Derbyshire views, an olde worlde garden, all mod. cons. indoors . . . '

'And a stairlift?'

'Not yet. I'm sure you'll put your mind to that! I believe you'll like the place, but if you don't we can move on somewhere else — Oh, and one more thing. How does 'Mrs. Bethany Tremaine' sound to you? Vaguely inviting, or horribly depressing?'

The heavens had already dropped to earth today. The globe had already paused its spinning. Could it really happen all over again?

He put an arm around me, and it seemed so very natural just to nestle into it. He was laughing at my confusion. I stammered, 'If — if that's meant to be a proposal of marriage

— it's a very unusual one!'

'I suppose I'm not a usual sort of person. But if you can put up with me — Bethany, I can't bear the thought of ever losing you . . .'

It was hard to take in all else he was saying. 'Rose Cottage' was there waiting for us. If I still wanted to continue nursing, of course I could do that: I could do anything, have anything, that it was in his power to lay in homage at my feet . . .

Well, maybe the flowery language was to be expected from a more or less distinguished man of letters. The depth of love I read in his grey, grey eyes meant far more.

In some limbo between joy and disbelief, I realised we had as witnesses an audience of furry, bewhiskered faces. I drew him a little way along the block of cabins.

'If I decide to say 'yes' . . . would there be room in your beautiful cottage for three? I want to adopt a cat. This cat!'

'*This* one? This hoary moth-eaten creature? Are you sure?'

'We owe her. Believe me.'

'We do? — if you say so, my love. Welcome to the happy family, pussy-cat!'

As Granny's rheumy eyes met mine through her wire door — the door that once I left so temptingly ajar for escape — I was positive the ancient animal gave me a knowing, toothless smile.

THE END

We do hope that you have enjoyed reading this large print book.

Did you know that all of our titles are available for purchase?

We publish a wide range of high quality large print books including:
Romances, Mysteries, Classics
General Fiction
Non Fiction and Westerns

Special interest titles available in large print are:
The Little Oxford Dictionary
Music Book, Song Book
Hymn Book, Service Book

Also available from us courtesy of Oxford University Press:
Young Readers' Dictionary
(large print edition)
Young Readers' Thesaurus
(large print edition)

For further information or a free brochure, please contact us at:
Ulverscroft Large Print Books Ltd.,
The Green, Bradgate Road, Anstey,
Leicester, LE7 7FU, England.
Tel: (00 44) **0116 236 4325**
Fax: (00 44) **0116 234 0205**

*Other titles in the
Linford Romance Library:*

ELUSIVE

Karen Abbott

Amelia has always been determined to marry for love . . . but with her elder brother dead and posthumously branded as a traitor, Amelia and her sister find themselves penniless and ostracised by society. When a relative contrives to put an 'Eligible Parti' under an obligation to make Amelia an offer, Amelia has to decide whether or not to stand by her principles . . . and face the consequences of turning down what might be her only chance to escape her unbearable situation.

MARRIED TO THE ENEMY

Sheila Holroyd

Faced with the choice of death or marriage to a stranger, Kate marries Lord Alvedon, the powerful servant of Queen Elizabeth. Taken away from everything she has ever known Kate finds it difficult to adjust to the strange new world of Elizabeth's court. Her innocence not only threatens her marriage, it puts her in great danger — and, unknown to her or her husband, a secret enemy plans to kill both of them . . .

TABITHA'S TRIALS

Valerie Holmes

Tabitha is reluctantly released from St Mary's Establishment for Impoverished Girls because Miss Grimley will not break the rules and allow her to remain. She must go into service, contributing to the school so that other girls will benefit. Tabitha rides on the back of a wagon and watches her past drift into the distance. With a heavy heart, she contemplates years of hard work and predictability stretching before her, little realising just what the future has to offer . . .

GENTLEMEN PREFER . . . BRUNETTES

Liz Fielding

Nick Jefferson can't resist a challenge, or a blonde! So when the latest platinum-haired woman to cross his path challenges him to cook her a romantic dinner, he accepts. Unfortunately Nick could burn water . . . Chef Cassie Cornwell is *not* Nick's type — she's a brunette, and the only woman to turn Nick down. She's disappointed he wants her to prepare a seduction feast rather than to share one. Unless Cassie can persuade him that blondes aren't necessarily more fun . . .

THE HONEY TREE

Glenis Wilson

Sparks fly when Merri Williams meets Walt Lime. She's struggling to keep Aunt Prue's riding stables afloat whilst Prue and Walt's Uncle Matt are in Dubai. To avoid bankruptcy, Merri buys more ponies and gives riding lessons to disabled children. But Walt is intent on stopping her. What is he concealing? And why has Prue gone to Dubai? 'When I return I'll tell you — until then you'll be on your own — promise you'll ask Walt for help . . . '